Briana,
I hope you enjoy this.
If not, I will have to

Borrachón

By Kevin Cullen

give Steve his money

back.

Your friend,
Kevin Cull

1

Based on characters by B. H. McCampbell.

Copyright © 2016 by Ulysses Media
All rights reserved.

ISBN-13: 978-1540804570

ISBN-10:1540804577

Also sold by Amazon Digital Services LLC

ASIN: B01NABVKVT

Dedicated to my wife, Jennifer, whose tender encouragement, steadfast support, and unconditional love were essential in the creation of this book.

Chapter 1

In the year 1884, Rio Bravo, Texas, was a new town, a growing town, and one with recognized prospects for success. Commerce, driven mostly by the country's hunger for beef, was thriving in the town and throughout the region. Rio Bravo's proximity to the Mexican border offered even more chances for prosperity, as well as danger in the forms of banditos and Mexican cattle rustlers. The town had a small bank, a hotel that was considered elegant given its surroundings, a restaurant, one saloon with a second about to open in the coming weeks, a livery, two food shops, a barber, and a funeral parlor.

It was nighttime, about 9:00 P.M., Sheriff John T. Chance and his deputy, Dude Warren, were walking down the main street of Rio Bravo, doing their nightly check to ensure that the doors of the various businesses were locked, that there were no signs of break-ins or any out-of-control rowdiness. The men, familiar with the recent tales of Dodge City, Tombstone, and Wichita, knew all too well what the combination of cowhands and cattle money could do to the peace of a town.

Sheriff Chance was 6 feet, 4 inches tall. He was large, with broad shoulders and while the years may have added pounds, he was sturdy and strong. The brim of his hat was more than slightly bent upward, he wore a beige vest over a worn plaid shirt. He was wearing a gun belt that contained a Colt revolver with a yellow pearl handle, carried near the back of his hip. He walked with a confident yet cautious swagger. Chance joined the Confederate Army at the age of 17 in 1863. Upon the surrender of the Confederacy two years later, he joined the U.S. Calvary, eventually achieving the rank of sergeant. He was stationed in the West Texas town of Fort Hood, on the border of Comancheria. During his service, he fought Comanches, Kiowas, and Apaches. After being in the Calvary for 15 years, he retired and moved to Rio Bravo, hearing about an opening for a sheriff. That was more than 5 years ago.

In comparison to Chance, Dude was slightly shorter and leaner. In direct contrast to the sheriff, he looked as if he put much more thought into his appearance. He wore a black cowboy hat with a sterling silver band and its brim was perfectly formed. He wore a black leather vest over a black cotton shirt. Unlike Chance, he carried two pistols: Colt Peacemakers with black handles. Dude was younger than Chance so he missed participation in not only the Civil War but in the Indian wars as well. His first real job was as a faro dealer in a sporting house in a sprawling town named Bufford in North Texas. Faro was a card game with simple rules and fast-paced waging. It was in Bufford that Dude was first exposed to shooting, learning mostly from a travelling gunman named Pete Dawkins. Dawkins liked faro and took a similar liking to Dude. Outside of gambling, neither of them partook in the other recreations offered in the house, like liquor or sporting women. Instead, they rode to the outskirts of town, practicing quick draws and perfecting their aims. When Dawkins went to push on, Dude joined him. The two eventually split up, with Dude arriving in Rio Bravo. Chance was actually the first person he met in the town. Along with Dude's familiarity in handling guns, Chance saw an inherent goodness in him.

As the two silently continue their walk, they saw two men come crashing out the Long Branch Saloon, wrestling and occasionally throwing punches. Chance and Dude picked up their pace and arrived just when the two men were rolling into the middle of the dirt street. The two men were obviously cowhands, dressed in chaps and dungarees. One was wearing a gun belt and the other was unarmed. Chance immediately pulled the armed cowhand off the man on the ground and spun him away. Dude helped the other one up but also grabbed him by the chest to restrain him. Cursing at Chance, the armed cowhand reached for his gun. But before the tip of the barrel completely cleared the holster, a shot was heard: he had been shot in his upper arm, the arm holding the gun. Dude, still restraining the other man with his right arm, was poised with a smoking gun in his left hand. Chance, realizing that he was the cowhand's intended target, stared at Dude with a look that combined amazement and gratitude. He also realized that his instinct to reach for his own pistol had completely abandoned him.

Chapter 2

The Sheriff's office and jailhouse was a one-story building, comprised of Chance's desk, a set of rifles, various Wanted posters on the wall, and two cells in the back. In one cell, the wounded cowhand was being bandaged by the town's doctor, Lamar Fix. In the other, the unarmed cowhand sat on the bunk, his head in his hands.

"It was the damnest thing I've ever seen," Chance was saying to the doctor. "It was as if Dude knew – knew beforehand – that he was gonna draw."

"Well, Chance, you always knew he was good," replied the doctor.

Chance shook his head and stared at the floor, "But not that good."

The cowhand being bandaged was Ned Burke, a drifter and saddle tramp not known for any cowboy skills in particular, recently hired by Nathan Burdette, the owner of the largest ranch in the territory. Burdette also owned the local feed store, was a trustee of the Rio Bravo City Bank, and was opening a new saloon in the town. Burke yelled, "He coulda blown my whole arm off!"

The doctor, moving the cigar in his mouth from one side to the other, was adept at ignoring complaining patients, especially ones as notoriously contemptible as Burke. "Actually," the doctor said to Chance, "The bullet went right into the middle – almost exactly, John T. – of the bicep. You could measure it. The bone stopped it. It's pretty shattered, as well."

John "Stumpy" Callahan entered the jailhouse; he walked with a pronounced limp. Stumpy owned a small – compared to his neighbors and the rest of southwest Texas – ranch about fifteen miles outside of Rio Bravo. Stumpy was the patriarch of one of the first families to settle in this section of Texas about twenty years ago. Coming from Missouri, he and his two sons had driven a small herd of cattle and settled outside of Rio Bravo. His wife, May-Anne, had died of cholera two years after they homesteaded. His oldest son, Malachy, was killed by Comanches in an attack two years later. Stumpy got his nickname during that attack, taking two arrows in his upper left thigh. His other son, Patrick, was killed by a stampede just last year. The unarmed cowhand from last night's fight, Joe Edwards, was Stumpy's ranch foreman.

Upon seeing Stumpy, Chance immediately stood up and put out his hand. "Why, Stumpy! How are ya? I think we got one of your hands here."

Stumpy, a man who tended to repeat – and sometimes mutter to – himself, said, "So I hear, John, so I hear."

Edwards jumped up to the cell bars, "I'm really sorry about this, Stump. I'll pay you back for bail and whatever else."

Stumpy looked at Edwards, his expression showed both sympathy and weariness. "Ah, don't fret upon it, Joe. I'm sure you was bullied into it." He turned to Chance, "Burdette's been trying to either hire Joe away, scare him off, and now I guess they wanna kill him. What is his bail, anyway?"

Chance leaned on his desk. "Oh, a night in jail will do it." He pointed to Burke. "He's the one in trouble: attempted assault on an officer of the law; possibly attempted murder; resisting arrest. I need a Marshall to sort it all out. And no bail for him." He unlocked Edwards's cell.

"Well, thankee, John. And you should know, I'm planning on a drive Monday week. With the beef price falling here, I'm going all the way up to Colorado Territory to market 'em. Know any good hands?"

"I thought you were well fixed for hands. What happened?" said Chance.

"Burdette happened," replied Stumpy. "Not only can he drive the local price down with all his beef, he either hired or scared away my best men. If I don't get more like Joe soon, it looks like I'll have to make the ride meself." He laughed at the thought of his taking an active part in a cattle drive, given his leg, age and the current state of his cowhand skills.

"Let's hope it don't come to that," replied Chance. "I'll keep my ears open for ya."

Just then, Dude entered the jailhouse. Upon seeing Stumpy, he grinned broadly, stuck out his hand, patted him on the back with the other and said, "Why, ol' Stump, I heard you was in town. I also heard you outrun your horse just to get here. Plan on ridin' back or are ya still not tired of walkin'? And ya gotta keep a closer eye on your boys here." He pointed his thumb at Joe.

Stumpy laughed and responded, "Oh, thanks for watching out for him, Dude. I'm obliged to you and John T. here. And the talk around the town already is about how you drew so fast on Burke."

Stumpy left with Joe. Chance turned to Dude, "Laredo stage supposed to get here by three. It should have a pack of warrants and posters for us. Mind meeting it? I have to send a wire requesting a Marshall."

"On my way, John T.," said Dude.

As Dude was heading toward the door, Burke yelled to him, "Another six inches to the right and ya woulda killed me!"

"But I wasn't aiming six inches to the right," responded Dude calmly. "I just wanted to get your attention. And thankfully, I did."

Chapter 3

The noon stage from Laredo arrived promptly at half past three. It stopped, as it always did, in front of the corral by Gibb's Livery Stables, allowing the horses to be cared for right away. Dude was waiting for the stage, leaning on a hitching rail, and whittling a stick to a sharp point. Two people got out of the stage: a tall man, about forty, wearing what most local people would consider "Sunday clothes"; the second was a woman, perhaps the prettiest woman Dude had ever seen. The woman was almost as tall as the man, with chestnut brown hair, swept up under a high-brimmed veiled blue hat. She wore a long blue dress with a bustle that had a large black ribbon tied in a bow in the back. Both were more than slightly drunk. The woman, despite the helping hand of the man as she descended the coach, almost lost her balance. The misstep made both of them laugh out loud. Once the woman righted herself, she and the man gathered their luggage from the shotgun rider and approached Dude.

"Hello, Sheriff," began the man, "could you point me in the direction of the Burdette Saloon?"

Numerous possible responses went through Dude's mind at once. The first was that the last thing either of these two people needed was more liquor. Another, more immediate, thought was to correct the misidentification of his title, although he felt some embarrassment, to the lady especially, that he was not the sheriff, "just" a deputy. He also discovered that he had instantly developed a profound jealousy of this man. He even briefly considered arresting them for public drunkenness.

Dude tipped his hat, mostly to the woman, and responded, "That's Deputy, not Sheriff, and everybody around here calls me 'Dude.' The Burdette Saloon, such as it is right now, is half-ways down the street on the left side."

"'Such as it is?'" asked the man.

"Yeah, it ain't finished yet," said Dude.

The man bit his lower lip. "Well, that is troubling. Mr. Burdette sent me a wire that it would be finished by now." He looked in the direction of the saloon briefly then turned back to Dude. "Oh, how rude of me, my name is Rudolph Trenton – Rudy to my friends, and this is Margaret Crenshaw – Maggie to her's." They both extended their hands to Dude.

"Well, it's a pleasure to meet you both and welcome to Rio Bravo," said Dude, shaking each of their hands in turn. "Around here we ain't too surprised the saloon's not done. We kinda have our own pace here. Unlike where y'all are from, which is...?" Dude felt his question sounded as if it was coming from a lawman, which it was. But he was relieved that the two were not married, at least not officially married. Common law marriages in the Southwest were very much just that: common. Women did not usually take the last name of their common law husbands.

Rudy smiled and said, "I've been hired by Mr. Burdette to run his new venture. Maggie and I are originally from St. Louis but we've both had experience setting up and running saloon businesses all over the Southwest. Perhaps our first stop should be the saloon to see for ourselves just how much progress has been made thus far."

Dude pointed them in the direction of the saloon and they parted, Maggie a bit unsteady. Maggie did turn back and gave Dude a glancing look as she and Rudy walked away. Suddenly feeling very self-conscious, Dude rubbed the stubble on his chin and contemplated a visit to Pedro the Barber.

Chapter 4

Dude was sitting back in the barber chair as Pedro finished shaving him. Chance walked in and asked about the Wanted posters.

"Damnit, John T., I forgot. Sorry. I'll get 'em right after this," said Dude.

"Too late. I got them myself. Anyway, from what I hear, you were preoccupied," said Chance.

"She's a looker alright," said Dude.

"And she may be a sporting girl," warned Chance.

"Naw, John, I think she's common law to that guy that's gonna run the Burdette Saloon," replied Dude.

"Well, it wouldn't be a first if she's both," said Chance. "Especially when times are tough."

"But times ain't tough right now," Dude responded. "In fact, they're kinda downright easy." Dude stood up and looked at himself in the barber's large mirror. "Great job once again, Señor," he said to Pedro, giving him a silver dollar. Dude turned to Chance, "How's our tenant?"

"Oh, he's sleeping now," responded Chance. "I don't expect to see Burdette coming around for him and he ain't got any friends, so we'll just wait for the Marshall."

"Okay, then, what's next? Too early for rounds. I can relieve you at the jail if you want."

"Other than having Burke, it is pretty slow. Why don't you take it easy for today?"

"Whatever you say, John T. You're the boss. Maybe I'll ride out and go see Stumpy for a game of checkers. Maybe bring him a bottle. He'll be by his lonesome once the drive's started. " He grabbed his hat, looked in the mirror to adjust it, and walked out.

Chance said to Pedro, "I could use a shave myself," and sat in the barber chair.

#

Out on the street, Dude walked into the Long Branch Saloon and up to the bar. "Hey, Dave," he said to the barman, "Gimme a bottle of whatever Stumpy drinks, will ya?"

Dave handed him a bottle of Irish whiskey, and said, "That's two dollars, Dude, expensive stuff, imported and all."

Dude placed the money on the bar and said, "That old gentleman's worth it, I guess."

Just as he turned to leave, Margaret Crenshaw, seemingly fully recovered from her tipsy state or perhaps working on a second wind, sitting at a table by herself with a bottle of champagne, called out, "Oh, Deputy, will you join me?"

Dude took off his hat and sat across from her. "You're in the wrong place, Miss Crenshaw, your bar is around the corner." He smiled at his own small joke.

"Well," she said, "It's not much of a bar right now. All sawdust and the sound of banging hammers. This gives me a chance to observe the competition. Would you like to join me for a drink?"

"I never developed a taste, Ma'am. Burns goin' down and sometimes comin' up. Like a branding iron. I'll take a beer maybe on occasion."

"Oh, this is different. It's champagne – or what passes for champagne this far south. It doesn't burn so much as caress." She poured a glass for Dude and edged it toward him.

Dude took a sip. "Why, that *is* different," he said. "Nicest liquor I ever come across. I could see people getting use to this." He drained the glass.

"Careful, Deputy," said Maggie. "This has been known to sneak up on one. And please call me Maggie, not Miss Crenshaw or 'Ma'am'. And why do they call you 'Dude'?"

"I guess it's because I dress better'n' most around here. A dude is kinda like a dandy. At least what passes for a dandy this far south." He grinned at the reuse of her own words. "But I never took offense. Mainly because no offense was ever meant by it. A couple of people said I looked like a dude and it kinda stuck."

Maggie looked over Dude's face. "You do kind of stick out around here. In a good way, I mean. I'm sure you get a lot of attention from the females."

Dude had never encountered a woman this forward and at once felt uncomfortable and attracted. His mind went over the few women he had known in his life. He never noticed – or perhaps never let himself notice – if any one of them had ever expressed a singular interest in him. That one girl in Buford accused him of being indifferent and preoccupied with dealing faro and developing his gun skills.

The touch of Maggie's hand on his brought him back to the present. "Dude, would you take me out riding some time? I haven't been on a horse since my teen years and want to see the countryside."

Dude saw his chance to find out about her situation. "I'd like to do that fine. Would Mr. Trenton be okay with that?"

"When it comes to business between Mr. Trenton and myself," replied Maggie, "it remains business. When it does not involve business, neither Mr. Trenton nor I concern ourselves with each other. This is not business. This is pleasure. My pleasure."

Dude stood and smiled, "Then it will be my pleasure, too. How about Sunday?"

Maggie returned his smile and offered her hand. "Sunday it is. Let us meet by the stable and you can help me choose a horse."

Dude put on his hat and turned to leave, almost forgetting Stumpy's whiskey.

Chapter 5

Stumpy sat on his porch playing an old mouth organ. The song was vaguely familiar: a peculiar combination containing strains of "My Darling Clementine" and "Green Sleeves." Dude rode up, tied his horse to the hitching post and walked down the pathway and through a white trellis studded with blooming yellow and red rose bushes on either side. He carried the bottle of Irish whiskey in his hand.

"Beware of Greeks bearing gifts," said Stumpy rising. He put down his harmonica on the small table that was situated between the two rocking chairs.

Dude laughed and said, "I ain't Greek so I guess you're safe, Stump," and handed Stumpy the bottle. Stumpy examined the label and smiled broadly.

"My brand, too," said Stumpy, "much obliged, Dude. Take a seat and I'll get us a couple of glasses."

"I'll take a seat but pass on the whiskey, thank you all the same." Dude sat in the chair opposite the one Stumpy just vacated.

Stumpy returned with the glasses, placed one in front of Dude and said, "Just in case ya change ya mind." Stumpy poured a drink into the glass he was holding and sat down.

"My father used to say, 'slainte' (pronounced "sal-ang-jee" in a Texas accent like Stumpy's), means 'health' or 'where's the next one?'" He laughed and downed the drink. Stumpy's laugh was more like a loud, uninhibited cackle.

Dude looked admiringly at the rose bushes. "Those are some pretty flowers, Stump."

"Yeah, my May-Anne planted those, oh, twenty years or so now. She was one for flowers. I always asked her to plant corn or spuds or somethin'. To use her gifts to feed me. And the boys." He paused while he thought of how much he missed all of them: his wife and two sons. He poured a second drink and stared at the flowers. "Yellow Rose of Texas. Ya know, that was written for a Negra woman. She was a spy for Texas who kept ol' Santa Ana occupied when Sam Houston's boys come to San Jacinto. Caught him with his pants down. Really!" He slapped his leg and cackled.

Dude smiled. "You know all those old Alamo stories, don't ya, Stump? Bowie and Crockett and them." He was attempting to get Stumpy to not dwell on the sadness of his late wife and sons.

Stumpy scratched at his beard and smiled. "Yeah, when I was a teenager, all them stories drifted back to Missor'. Ya'd think they was gods killed behind them walls. Ya know, it was one of the reasons why I always wanted to come to Texas. To live among legends, even it was just among the ghosts of legends. But it ain't real, none of it. Just stories. Give something enough time, the realness gets replaced with myth. Like the facts get boiled away and all you're left with it is a fairy tale." He looked at the rose bushes again.

Stumpy poured himself another drink, again offering one to Dude, who once more declined.

"How do you drink that stuff? It burns my throat somethin' awful."

"This is smooth compared to some of the stuff I had. The day I hired Joe he had tequila and we toasted. Toasted? My belly was the only thing that got toasted." He cackled again. "Damn! No, this is mother's milk to that. Now, I don't know how them Mex'cans take it. But you're smart staying away from it, Dude. All of it. There was a time when I thought it would fill a hole of sadness somewhere deep in my insides but it never did. It sometimes even made the hole deeper. So I stopped trying to fill that hole with whiskey."

"Then why the hell do you drink it now?" said Dude.

"For the taste, ya idiot!" Stumpy let out a loud, long cackle.

Chapter 6

To Dude, Sunday came slowly but it was finally here. Dude, dressed all in black with the silver band around his black hat, stood outside Gibbs' stable. He had left his guns in the jail. The extra forty-five minutes that it took Maggie to show up seemed to drag on as slow as the days since they first made the date. When she appeared, wearing ankle-high brown suede gaucho pants, long black boots, a blue denim blouse and red scarf, she did not apologize for being late. Dude would have waved off an apology anyway.

"Are you an experienced horse trader, Dude?" Maggie said. "I will need some guidance so I won't get swindled."

"Oh, I've known Gibbs since I moved here. He sold me this quarter horse," replied Dude. "Gibbs is fair but makes a living, if you know what I'm getting at."

Gibbs came out of the stable. He was a tall man with a stocky build. He was a blacksmith as well as the stable owner. "Why, hay-low, Dude. How can I help ya today?" Gibbs had an unusual accent that was a mixture of Dutch and Texas drawl.

Dude stuck out his hand and Gibbs shook it. "Mr. Gibbs, this here is Miss Crenshaw and she is looking for a riding pony."

Gibbs extended his hand to Maggie and looked her up and down. "Evah rode be-far? Ya look like ya know your way around ta horse."

Maggie replied, "Mr. Gibbs, I've been riding since I was a little girl in St. Louis. I'm looking not for a fast horse like Dude's but a more elegant, thoroughbred that can go long distances. What do you have like that?"

Gibbs escorted the two of them through the stable of horses until they came to a gray and white Appaloosa mare. "How's dis one?" he said, "She's two years old, very gentle. Because you're a friend of the Deputy: dirty dollars."

Maggie laughed. "Thirty dollars? What would it be if I wasn't a friend of the Deputy? I'd hate to think of that price?"

Dude blushed. He did not like haggling. And he especially did not like haggling for another person when his name got dragged into it. "Tell ya what, Gibbs. I got a twenty dollar gold piece burning a hole in my pocket and it's yours, straight up trade."

Gibbs scratched at the three-day old stubble on his face. He looked at Dude, then at Maggie before speaking. "Wahl, I guess ta difference will be made up when I tell Mrs. Gibbs ta news about Dude's new girl! Tat's a deal. Now what about saddle and tack? I got some dat'll fit a fine lady natural."

For an extra ten dollars, Gibbs provided a used, newly polished brown leather Western saddle, bit and reins, and a wool blanket. Dude gave him the twenty-dollar gold piece and two five-dollar notes and they shook hands. Throughout the entire transaction, Maggie never offered to pay or even thank Dude, as if it was all expected. If anything, she seemed impatient and annoyed.

They rode east out to the banks of the Rio Grande. Maggie rode well, as Gibbs had assumed. She stood straight in the saddle and handled the new horse as if she had owned it for years. They stopped and dismounted. Dude took out his canteen and offered it to Maggie. She took a drink and handed it back. Then she reached into her hip pocket and produced a flask. She pointed it towards Dude but he smiled and waved it back.

"Oh, that's right," said Maggie, "like a branding iron. Well, how's this?" She took a drink from the flask and bent in to kiss Dude on the mouth. He returned the kiss and smiled. In that moment, an image that Dude had been suppressing since he first saw Maggie came rushing toward him with the speed and power of a bullet fired from a gun. For the first time, he allowed the image to fully materialize. It was an image of him and Maggie together, living like a couple. He allowed himself to see it and feel it. He allowed himself to imagine that he finally was complete, a whole man. A man who had finally found everything, even love.

Even though his mind was intensely focused on that single image and all the potential joy it held, Dude felt that he still needed to appear fully composed. "Well, that certainly cooled it," he managed to say. "Gives your kiss a nice fire, too," he added.

Maggie smiled and said, "That is just the beginning of my thank you for the horse and saddle." She kissed him again and reached for his crotch. She caressed his manhood through his pants. They lay down on the grassy banks of the Rio Grande and made love while the rushing waters poured over the boulders and rocks in the near distance.

Chapter 7

Stumpy Callahan knew from experience that a cattle drive was an ambitious undertaking that required planning and the coordination of many parts. Some experienced ranchers have said that it takes as much time preparing and mapping the drive as it does to carry it out. Stumpy was about to have eleven men, most of them complete strangers, embark on an almost eight-hundred-mile journey transporting more than two thousand head of steer. Along the route, there could be Indians in the form of Kiowa and Comanche, Mexican bandits, and perhaps even white men planning a rustling raid. Stumpy, who could never be described as religious, prayed that the men would make the trip – and return – unharmed. Indians could be bargained with, and pockets of known and past dangers can be avoided with the proper planning. No one except Stumpy knew of the desperation of the drive. He had mortgaged his land in order to raise the funds to get men and supplies for the trip. If it failed, he was finished. But if not religious, Stumpy was inherently optimistic.

Being the middle of September, the timing of the drive was in Stumpy's favor. The heat of the summer would be over and the rains would not come until late October. Stumpy went as far as checking the Farmer's Almanac for weather forecasts for the region. According to the Almanac, September through mid-October should be dry and relatively cool.

Joe Edwards had personally recruited five cowhands who would make the drive with him. Foremost in the qualifications was no past association with Nathan Burdette. Nathan was the person who would benefit the most from a failed drive. He would surely make a play to acquire Stumpy's land and extend his own spread. If he could infiltrate the drive's hands with any of his own men, he could almost guarantee a failure. Joe rode out as far as Corpus Christi to find and hire hands for the drive. One was a cousin of Joe's and two others were ex-lawman. The best of them were two experienced hands who had been on longer drives with larger herds. Another cowboy on the drive was a rancher who was volunteered by his mother just to help her old friend Stumpy. Upon arriving at Stumpy's ranch, he even demonstrated his skills around cooking on an open fire. Stumpy also enlisted two local brothers who had little experience but were very willing and who seemed to be able to take orders. His own hired man volunteered to drive the supply wagon, cook, and perform other auxiliary tasks.

Applying the adage that the shortest distance between any two points is a straight line, Stumpy and Joe mapped out a trail that went to Las Animas County, Colorado as straight as possible but that also allowed for water and open ground for grazing. Joe had gotten all the required supplies – based on Stumpy's exhaustive list – in town, avoiding, of course, any purchases from a Burdette-owned business.

The night before they were to head out, Stumpy sat down with Joe for some last minute instructions, several of which he had stated many times before. "Above all else, Joe," began Stumpy, "protect those men. Make sure they all got repeaters. If the Kiowas don't wanna talk turkey, six-guns will scare 'em away, even if you just keep shootin' in the air. And you got a couple of Mexicans to talk your way outta most trouble with banditos. Stay clear of other herds: you don't want any mixed brands that may set y'all up as rustlers." When he was finished, he handed Joe a solid gold ring with a design of two hands holding a heart. "This was my mother's. They started calling it a Claddagh back home. It's supposed to symbolize love," Stumpy let out a small cackle, "but it also means friendship. And luck. I want you to have it, Joe. For luck. And besides, if the money I gave ya runs out, maybe you can get a couple of greenbacks for it." He patted Joe on the back and went off to his room. "Good night, Joseph."

#

The group started out at sunrise the next morning, a Monday. If they kept their intended pace, they would reach the outskirts of Las Animas within five weeks. Joe, at the front the herd, had the

Claddagh ring on a piece of twine around his neck and tucked securely underneath his shirt. At the end of the herd, the cook drove the chuck wagon obediently onward. The wake of dust was so thick that not a single hoof of cow or horse could be seen.

Chapter 8

It was dusk when Joe had the herd stopped. They had made about almost twenty miles that day, a significant distance considering the daily allowance of two stops for grazing and rest. At this rate, Joe figured, they could be in Las Animas in less than four weeks. He assigned young Milburn Palmer (he preferred "Burny" to "Millie") to watch the herd that night. Burny had been handpicked by Stumpy himself and was as reliable as nightfall. He originally signed on as a cook – he did wonders with chicken and barbecue – but he was as adept to cowboying as he was to cooking. Roping especially came easy and natural to him, and he could ride like no one Joe had ever seen. Burny had a wife and three little ones on his own small ranch back in Sabinal but took this job because his mother knew Stumpy from Missouri. When his mother had heard about Stumpy's troubles, especially the death of his son, Patrick, she wrote him a letter offering the services of her boy. Even though Stumpy eventually wrote back that he would never feel right to put another young man in such danger, Milburn arrived, frying pan and ropes in hand. He signed on the drive and refused any payment.

Along with Milburn, Joe had signed Burtrum Hayes and Harper Turner both from San Angelo; Otis Walker from Abilene; Pedro "Pete" Gomez from Laredo; George Walsh from Midland; Ted Davis from Oklahoma; and Bradford and Taylor Beaverson from Rio Bravo. Hayes and Turner had both been on David Morrill Poor's Chihuhua Trail drive in '68. Joe thought that their experience on that drive, longer than this one by almost 400 miles, would be a big asset. Walker was an old friend of Joe's, cousins actually, and had cowboyed together since they were teenagers. Gomez was an old ranch hand who had been on drives from Texas to Kansas. Walsh was once a Texas Ranger and fought Kiowas and Comanches along the Brazos; the story goes that he had a fistfight with William "Bigfoot" Wallace and forced to leave the Rangers. Davis was an ex-Pinkerton Detective who quit for better pay as a cowhand; he usually rode point but swapped with Walsh when tiredness and nerves got the better of him. The local Beaverson brothers, seventeen and sixteen, were on their first drive but were well known in town for being good horsemen; their father, Frank, had died of influenza the past winter. Driving the supply wagon was Diego Morales, Stumpy's own hired man whose regular job included tending the land, especially May-Anne's roses.

While Burny rode off to watch and sing to the cattle, Joe and Diego started a fire and prepared dinner. Stumpy had provided enough beef to last the drive but also a large wired crate with a dozen live chickens so "the boys won't get sick of lookin' at, wet-nursing and eatin' the same thing day in and day out." Burny had supplied two jugs of his barbecue sauce that went well with chicken or beef. Of course, there were beans and corn and taters, as well as canned peaches. Diego brought along three coffee pots. There were two large wooden barrels of water even though the trail Stumpy and Joe laid out had plenty of water sources. Pete stated that this was the best-supplied drive he had ever been a part of, even the one-thousand mile Fort Worth to Abeline drives along the Chisolm trail that he had hired onto. Those drives had twice as many cattle and men, and covered an additional five hundred miles. Stumpy was one to spoil his men, especially if he was not riding along with them.

After dinner, Joe sent the older Beaverson boy to relieve Burny and then settled in for the night. When he closed his eyes, he saw the hindquarters and tails of cattle. He drifted off in the hopes of another twenty-mile day.

Chapter 9

The herd was just passing into northern Texas on the trail to Colorado. There was a thick, curved forest of high cottonwoods to the right that seemed to slowly drift behind the herd as it passed. Joe had Ted Davis on point and placed Milburn Palmer in the first wing position on the right of the herd. Joe had decided to have the Beaverson boys ride flank behind Milburn, with the elder Bradford in front of his brother, Taylor. Behind Taylor, on the end of the right side, riding drag, was Harper Turner. Harper's counterpart on the left side was Otis Walker, and directly in front of Otis was Burtrum Hayes on one flank. Completing the left side was George Walsh and Pete Gomez. Besides the Beaverson boys, George had the least cowhand experience of anyone in the outfit. Joe figured that by putting him between two veteran hands like Burtrum and Pete, any mistakes could be kept to a minimum. Diego Martinez was driving the wagon and extra horses on the left side of the herd.

Joe rode up to George Walsh and said, "On the left, George."

George looked up and said, "Hey, Trail Boss. Want me to swap with Ted for now?"

Joe replied, "No, no. Just wanna know about the area we're heading into. And please call me 'Joe.'"

George nodded and said, "Well, the danger's behind us where I figure. Comanch' are on the reservation comin' into Oklahoma. Should be clear."

"Just what I wanted to hear. Thanks. And relieve Ted in a couple of miles if you would." With that, Joe rode up to Pete Gomez riding wing on the left.

Pete greeted Joe, "Hey, Boss. I been meaning to tell you that if I remember right, I think there is a good place for camp less than two miles northeast. Big grass, between two streams. Flat."

Joe pushed his hat back on his head. "Pete, first off, you can call me 'Joe', 'José', anything but 'Boss' or worse yet, 'Jefe.' But that's good news. Go catch up to Ted and get them headed that way. And see how's he doing. I'll take your spot here."

"Right, Boss – I mean Joe," said Pete and galloped to catch up to Ted.

Harper Turner called out to Taylor Beaverson, who was responsible for the portion of the herd just ahead of him, "Don't turn your back on them cattle, son. Seeing a horse's tail can spook 'em or insult 'em. Either way, ya don't wanna deal with the results."

In response, Taylor raised his left hand, the one carrying his rope, and turned his horse around.

It was coming on dusk when the first arrow hit. That one landed in Harper Turner's left shoulder blade. The second in his right kidney. The third in the hindquarter of one of the steer for which he was responsible. Then the arrows came as steady and random as raindrops from a sun shower. Three more cattle were hit. Harper's horse was hit in its side. Another arrow appeared in Harper's left calf, as if it grew directly from it. Harper's section of the herd, the lower right portion, scattered and stampeded. Harper Turner fell from his horse and was dead before he hit the ground.

Otis Walker was responsible for the portion of the herd to the left of Harper Turner's. He saw Harper's steers careening into his own and immediately yelled, "Turner, what the hell ya doin'?" Not seeing him in his usual space, Otis turned and tried to keep his own steers together. An arrow punctured his neck and Otis Walker was killed immediately. That section of the herd stampeded.

Pete Gomez and Burtrum Hayes, on the left side of the herd, saw the rear sections charging and scurrying. They rode back and the two of them turned as many of the panicking cattle they could to the right. Those steer, in running into the other sections of the herd, spooked those cattle and the stampede was on. "Turn 'em! Turn 'em!" they both yelled.

Burny Palmer, on the upper right side of the herd, felt the change in direction almost instantaneously. He immediately rode back to tell Bradford Beaverson, the cowboy directly behind him on the right side, to take his place at the front and he would get to his younger brother, Taylor, and instruct him on what to do with the change of direction and increased speed of the herd. Burny galloped at full speed, standing up in his saddle, waving his right arm to indicate the direction he wanted Taylor to move, all the time yelling to Taylor to circle out and allow the herd to run to the right. Taylor, in the confusion, and despite his experience as an equestrian, pulled the reins of his horse too hard and too suddenly. His horse reared and he fell. The horse quickly sped out of harm's way but Taylor Beaverson was trampled to death by the rushing steer.

Joe had been riding alongside the wagon, he saw the commotion and told Diego to follow the herd and to stay on its left side. He then rode behind the herd and pulled out his pistol, firing it in the air to urge the cattle to the right. Burny was behind the herd, too, coming from the right side.

"Joe, where's Harper? Where the hell is Harper?" Burny shouted.

Joe slowed his horse. "Dunno," he shouted back. "Somethin' musta happened. Let's wear 'em out and we'll backtrack later." The two got behind the herd, firing their pistols in the air and hollering.

Once the herd was out of range, the rain of arrows stopped.

Exhausted, the herd finally stopped as well, almost as one. The herd had run past the spot Pete had suggested by a couple of miles. Still, the area was grassy and water was reachable. Ted Davis was the first to dismount. George Walsh and Pete Gomez then came riding up and dismounted. George bent over and vomited. Pete threw himself to the ground in exhaustion. Bradford Beaverson was next to appear. He stayed on his horse. Milburn Palmer, Burtrum Hayes, and Joe Edwards came riding up slowly together. Burt rode up to Bradford and spoke to him quietly. Then Bradford dismounted, followed by Burtrum. Joe and Burny both dismounted and took the saddles off their horses.

Joe was the first to speak. "When the wagon gets here, we'll make camp and change horses. George, you and Ted will head back out with me. I need Burtrum and Bradford to stay here. Pete, you and Burny take a head count. I know we lost some but I need to know just how many. And everybody get your rifles out."

When Diego came with the wagon and extra horses, everyone set to work on making camp. No one was hungry but Diego started a campfire. He put on all three pots of coffee.

Just before nightfall, Joe, George and Ted saddled up their fresh horses and rode out to the area they had all just come from.

They came upon Taylor Beaverson's trampled body first. He lay in mud, perhaps six inches beneath the level ground. It was hard to tell the difference between the yellowish-blue bruises on his exposed body parts and the greenish-blue of the decay of death.

Joe looked at both George and Ted. "Any chance we can preserve the body and bring it with us to take back?"

George shook his head and answered, "Sorry, Joe. Just not practical. We got to bury him here."

Joe whistled through his teeth. "Yeah, thought so. Just thought you two may have known a way. I got his brother and his mother to answer to..." He trailed off.

Ted looked at the body. "We can at least bring him back to the camp. Bury him by that stream maybe. I'll put him on my horse." Ted tried to lift the body by himself. Taylor had been a thin, lanky kid but the extra weight of the dried and drying mud added at least an extra thirty pounds. Seeing that Ted was having trouble, Joe grabbed Taylor's body under the arms and Ted grabbed the legs. The two of them carried and draped Taylor Beaverson's body over Ted's horse, behind the rear part of the saddle.

They rode on until they found Harper Turner's body. The arrows in his back and leg acted as markers. When they rode up to the body, the earth around him was soaked with his blood, making dark purple mud. George dismounted first. He removed the arrow from Harper's calf. He placed it on the ground then removed the one from the kidney, and finally the one in the back. Exactly the reverse order of the way they came.

Joe dismounted and walked through the purplish mud. "Can you tell anything by the arrow? Like tribe or somethin'?" he asked George.

George looked at Joe. "An arrow's an arrow, Joe. Anyone who says they can tell a tribe by the arrowheads or whatnot is either a liar or a fool. What is strange is that they didn't chase us down. They couldn't have been firing from horseback, I can tell ya that. Any Comanch' brave can shoot from a horse and be dead accurate. And if they can't, they don't pass the warrior test. These arrows probably came from that line of trees over there." He pointed at the cottonwoods.

Ted pulled his Scofield rifle out of its scabbard and dismounted. He cocked the rifle and said, "Okay, then, let's take the body and get outta here. I'll cover."

Joe did not move right away. "Maybe they just wanted beef."

George shook his head. "No, they hit what they shoot at, generally. And if they was just after beef, they wouldn't leave all that." He swept his hand across a section in the near distance that contained at least three dead steer, each with arrows sticking out of them. "I'll take Harper." George picked up Harper Turner's body, stiff with rigor mortis, placed it over his left shoulder, and draped it on the back of his horse.

The three men rode west in the general direction that Otis Walker would have been before the stampede. Unlike Harper, the fatal arrow did not serve as a marker. It took them almost thirty minutes to find the body. Otis Walker had fallen forward and the front of the arrow had snapped off probably on impact with the ground.

George again dismounted first. He had been calm and matter-of-fact until that point. "Mother of God!" he said. "I ain't never seen anything like this in my whole life. Poor sonovabitch."

Joe dismounted, walked over to the body and whispered, "I'm sorry, Cousin Otis," then gently and firmly lifted the body and draped it over his own horse. The three steered back in the direction of the new campsite.

Upon arriving at the camp, Bradford came running up to Ted's horse. He looked at his brother's motionless body. Tears burned the rims of his eyes. He looked at Ted and whispered, "I was hoping…maybe…he's tough. What am I gonna tell our mother?"

Joe dismounted and walked over to Bradford. "I'm sorry, Brad. I shouldn't have put you on the same side. I don't know what I was thinking. I am so sorry."

Bradford looked at Joe. "Mr. Edwards…Boss…it wasn't nothin' you did. Whether we was on separate sides, next to one another, it wouldn't have mattered. I guess it just happened."

Burtrum walked up to George's horse and examined the body draped over the back of it. "Jesus, Pard, how many times did they get you? Shit." His eyes filling with tears, he pulled the body gently from the horse and laid it on the ground.

Both Diego and Pete walked slowly up to Otis's body and together they placed him on the ground. They both made signs of the cross.

Joe turned from Bradford. "We'll dig graves and bury them in the morning. Right now, we need a meeting."

They all – except for Burny who was nighthawking the herd – gathered around the fire Diego had made earlier. Joe was the only one to stand. "Okay, Pete, what's the count?"

Pete answered, "We only lost about three dozen or so, Joe."

Joe nodded. "Well, that's good. But we still only got seven hands for almost two thousand head. Burtrum, can that be done?"

Burtrum Hayes thought for a moment. "Yeah, Joe," he said. "It'll be hard but I think it can be done. We'll have to spread out more, naturally, cut the herd into bigger sections. But keep the same pace. It will be the damndest drive I ever been on, I'll tell ya that. We'll all have stories to tell back home."

Joe looked at Bradford Beaverson. "What about you, Brad? Think you can go on?"

Bradford stared at the fire for what seemed like a long time. "Sure, Joe, I can go on," he finally said. It marked the first time he had referred to Joe Edwards as "Joe."

Ted broke up a long stick and threw the pieces in the fire. He asked the group, "What are the choices? Turn the herd back? We've done a good few days, maybe almost a quarter of the way, by my reckoning. And we'd have to go back through whatever that hell that was today."

Joe looked at the group. "Ted's got a good point. We're making good time. Or at least we *were*. What are the other choices?"

George spit a large amount of tobacco juice into the fire and said, "We could eat 'em." A couple of the cowboys laughed.

When Diego added, "Don't ask me to cook 'em!" a couple more laughed.

Chapter 10

Nathan Burdette walked into the jailhouse. Dude looked up from the cigarette he was rolling and yelled to the back of jail, "Burke, ya got a visitor!"

Burdette laughed dryly and looked at Dude. "I'm not here to see him, Deputy. I came by to invite you and the Sheriff to the grand opening of my saloon tonight."

Chance stood up from his desk and said to Burdette, "Thanks just the same, Burdette, but I think you'll only see me there if there is any trouble. Which I hope there isn't."

Dude smiled at Burdette, and said, "And since I don't drink it looks like the Rio Bravo law enforcement won't be represented there tonight. Unless, as Chance says, there's trouble."

Burdette smiled back at Dude, "For someone who doesn't drink, Deputy, I hear you spend a lot of time at my new place."

Chance interjected quickly to change the subject, "I would think, Burdette, that you would have at least some interest in your employee, or former employee. The fact is he's being picked up by a U.S. Marshall today."

Burdette looked at Chance, "I suspect, Sheriff, that by the time I'm finished, everybody in this town will either be an employee or a former employee of mine in one capacity or another. Including yourself. Well, if either or both of you change your mind, my invitation stands. Good day, gentlemen." Burdette left the office.

Dude looked up at Chance, "Is it just me or do you hear a rattle every time that guy enters and leaves a room?"

Burke yelled from his jail cell, "I'm gonna tell him you said that!"

Dude yelled back at Burke, "Shut-up in there. You'll probably never see him again in this lifetime. And it's clear Burdette doesn't give a flea's ass whether you live or die." To Chance, he said, "I won't be missing him a lick," and pointed his thumb to the cell.

Chance smiled and shook his head. "Burdette does have a point about you going back and forth from that saloon of his. People see things. And they talk."

Dude stood up. "Has it affected this job a single ounce? Don't I still make my rounds and do everything you expect? Just because you choose to..."

Dude was interrupted by the arrival of U.S. Marshall Charlie Smith. Charlie almost filled the doorway. He was taller than Chance and outweighed him by at least twenty pounds. Chance walked over and gave Charlie a hearty handshake.

"Well, Charlie! How have ya been?" said Chance as he patted him on the back. "And you remember Dude?"

Dude stood up and shook Charlie's hand, "My god, have you got even taller since the last time I seen ya?"

Charlie laughed good naturedly, and replied, "Hello, Dude, you still got that quarter horse what can outrun lightening?"

Chance said to Charlie, "Your prisoner's over here and I've got the charges written out along with my and Dude's statements. Do you think that'll be enough or will we have to ride out to Laredo to testify?"

"Not sure, John," said Charlie. "They're getting kind of peevish over there. May want ya in person. I take it you'd have to do it separately needing to have one person watch the store so to speak."

"Yeah, that would have to be the way," said Chance. "Do you have time for a drink, Charlie?" He turned to Dude and said, "Dude, ya mind?"

"Watch the store so to speak?" said Dude. "Go ahead, John T. With our time together getting so short, I'm happy to look after Burke."

Chance and Charlie walked out the door and towards the saloon. "Oh, John," said Charlie, "I saw our pal Rocky Ryan a while back. He said to say hello."

Chance laughed. "He's a good man, Rocky. Good shot from what I remember."

Charlie said, "Speaking of good shots, is Dude still just as fast?"

Chance shook his head, "If not faster. Up until now he's been the only extra hand I needed. Hell, he's been like having a second sheriff. Sure he's fast but he's also smart and tough."

Charlie said, "What do you mean, 'Up until now?'"

They had reached the saloon and walked up to the bar. They ordered whiskey. Chance began, "Well, lately, it's been a woman, the wrong type of woman in my opinion. Anyway, Dude's been keeping company with her. And there's no talking to him."

Charlie sighed and said, "There usually never is when a man gets like that. He becomes like a kid again." They clinked glasses and drank and Charlie said, "Well, let's have one more, then I should go. I gotta get back to Laredo with your man there before nightfall. Next time we'll sit and eat too. Or if ya have to come to Laredo, we can catch up some more then." The two men shook hands and headed back to the jailhouse.

#

In the jailhouse, Charlie was reviewing the charges while Dude handcuffed Burke's hands. Charlie looked at Burke and said, "What happened to his arm? They'll ask."

Chance replied, "Dude had to shoot him, he didn't have a choice."

Dude said, "Yeah, you could say I dis-armed him," and smiled.

Burke spat at Dude and said, "You won't be laughing the next time I see ya, ya son-of-a-bitch!"

Dude looked at Charlie, "Oh, you two are gonna have a fun journey together."

Charlie smiled, looked down at the papers Chance had handed him and said, "Okay, the 'Attempted Murder of a Peace Officer' and the 'Assault of a Peace Officer' may be enough to keep you lads home. Shame, though, cuz I would miss the chance of buying you both a steak."

They all walked outside and Dude helped Burke get up on a horse while Charlie mounted his own horse.

Dude and Chance each shook Charlie's hand and wished him luck.

With his hands cuffed behind him and mounted on the horse, Burke said, "I didn't assault nobody!"

As Charlie led Burke's horse, Dude turned to him and said, "Too bad we can't handcuff his mouth!"

Chapter 11

The sun had been up for an hour. Diego read over the three graves. He read from a Spanish Bible, the only one in the camp. When he was done, the eight remaining cowhands on the drive mounted their horses. Already that morning, they had dug three graves, packed up and broke camp.

Joe addressed them from horseback, "Okay, you know where you're supposed to be. Ted, on point again. Let's get some miles behind us and aim to stop around noon. Now let's get 'em out and movin.'"

Once the herd was moving north again, Joe took the flanker place held by Taylor Beaverson the day before. He was on the right side of the herd, between Taylor's brother, Bradford, on the wing in front of him, and Pete Gomez behind him riding drag. This way, Joe figured, he could keep an eye on Bradford and not have to worry about what may be going on behind him because Pete was so experienced. However, he was concerned about Pete's exposure to the troubles that befell Harper Turner and Otis Walker. That was why he placed George Walsh, the former Texas Ranger and veteran Indian fighter, to Pete's left on the other drag position. In front of George, he asked Burtrum Hayes to flanker the mid-left section of the herd. In front of Burtrum was Burny Palmer: reliable and one of the most agreeable, most selfless people he had ever met. Joe did not allow himself to think too long or too hard on what he would have to tell Burny's mother or Stumpy if anything were to happen to Burny. Joe had Diego place the wagon and extra horses to the right of the herd to keep him in his constant view.

Joe had instructed George to drop back to the rear of the herd every couple of miles and check for anyone who might be following them. The plan for the trail had changed so that the herd avoided any lines of trees or other areas that could provide cover for unwanted attackers. The change made the trail more difficult and may prove to add more days to the drive but Joe thought it necessary.

George had ridden behind the herd a few times when he thought he spotted riders in the distance behind him. His horse bucked slightly. "You smell it, too, Honey?" he whispered to the horse. He took out his spyglass and confirmed that a group of more than a dozen men were heading east. He did not see any Indians among them. Was this a different bunch then the ones that attacked yesterday, George asked himself. George stopped and thought for a moment: should he ride after them and investigate or go on with the herd and warn Joe? His Ranger instincts were telling him to wade right into the bastards. But if he missed them or overshot their location, they could outflank the herd on the right. It never occurred to him that he could not outfight a dozen men or that Joe could be short one more hand. George decided to hold back, trail the herd and tell Joe when they stopped at noon. Being directly behind the herd until then would give him the best chance to react if there was an attack.

Ted found a grazing spot a few minutes after noon and the herd was stopped. One by one, each hand went to Diego's wagon to switch horses. While Joe was saddling up his fresh mount, George rode up to him.

"Joe," George began, "a group passed under us about eight miles back. A dozen, at the least. I didn't see any Indians."

Joe stopped in the middle of tightening his saddle. "Different bunch?"

"Not sure," said George. "If it was white men shooting arrows, that would explain why they didn't go after the meat or attack on horseback. But if it's the herd they want and they got us outnumbered why didn't they just charge?"

Joe looked at George. "Pick us off over time maybe. Got any suggestions?"

George answered quickly, "I've been thinking. Let me fall back and track 'em. If they set up for something, I can get a couple, maybe even spook 'em. Problem is, for both them and me, is that we're now in open country. I don't know how they're gonna deal with that if they're planning something. If they charge, you'll have to prepare – maybe keep the wagon between them and the herd – then we can maybe get them in a crossfire. I think that's the best thing. If it turns out to be nothin', all you got to lose is that you're down one hand while I track 'em. The other thing I was thinkin' is to leave me here to snipe 'em. Problem with that is what if they ain't the bunch what attacked yesterday? What if they're just riding through? No, I think trackin' is the best idee. Keep 'em honest if they honest and catch 'em in the act if they ain't."

Joe thought for a moment, weighing George's plan. "Just you? Is that – is that alright with you?"

George smiled, "Oh, hell-shit, Joe, I been outnumbered before. And by a lot more. I'm just relieved they ain't Comanch'. And to keep this herd moving, you need all the hands you got. Besides, no one here's used to this type of thing. And you know I'm a better fighter than cowhand. You're just too polite to say it out loud." He smiled broadly.

Joe smiled back. "Alright then. Tellin' ya to be careful is like tellin' the sun to be bright. And thank you." He stuck out his hand.

George shook it discreetly. "If nothin' happens – and I hope it don't – I'll find you and the herd tonight."

George went to get his other horse. Joe called Burtrum Hayes over. "Burt," he said quietly, George saw a bunch what may be followin'. He's gonna check 'em out. I need you to drop back and kinda do his position and yours. True drag position. Okay?"

Burtrum searched Joe's face for signs of anxiousness. He nodded, mounted up and rode off to get in place.

George mounted and rode perpendicular to the herd, heading east. He saw a line of scrub pine trees in the distance and headed for it. Once there, he tied up his horse inside the sparse woods, about twenty yards from the clearing, took off the saddle and took his Winchester rifle from its scabbard. He carried the saddle to the beginning of the line of trees, laid it on the ground and lay behind it. His checked his rifle, placed it next to him, and pulled out a pouch of chewing tobacco. He put a wad in his mouth and laid his head on the saddle.

After twenty minutes or so of chewing and spitting, he heard the group approaching. They were about two-hundred yards below and across from him. He turned over, placed his chin on the saddle and watched them ride by. He counted twenty-two men, all white. He used his spyglass and saw that almost half of the men had bows slung behind their backs. "Sonovabitch," he whispered softly to himself.

When they had passed about a mile in front of him, George got up, picked up his saddle, and walked back to his horse. His horse had just relieved himself and George said quietly, "Good idea." He went further in the woods, dropped his pants and moved his bowels. Coming back to saddle his horse, he whispered, "Now we'll both be lighter." George walked the horse along the tree line as far as the cover lasted. He could still see the men in the distance, which meant that if he went into the open, they could see him as well. He waited until they were completely out of site. Then he mounted and followed them.

Since it did not have a herd to move, the group could ride faster. George, on his own, kept a pace similar to that of the herd. That way, if the group set up for an ambush, George should be directly across from the herd. The pace also helped George to keep from being detected by the group. George thought that they were waiting until they could find cover before setting up. But with the new route staked out by Joe and Ted, there should not be any cover, at least not for another day's ride or more. As planned, the openness was protecting the herd, but it was also beginning to frustrate George as he wanted to take action as soon as possible. The bows had all but confirmed that this was the group that killed Taylor, Harper and Otis, and George wanted justice. Patience was never part of George's make-up and the lack of it was partially the reason he was no longer a Texas Ranger. His "disagreement" with Bigfoot Wallace was over Bigfoot's insistence that the Rangers not chase down a rogue band of Comanches. That band, George learned afterward, attacked an Army supply wagon later that day, killing four soldiers and stealing a buckboard full of rifles and ammunition.

The group may have started to get frustrated as well. They had stopped and dismounted. George pulled up himself and rode back, out of the group's line of sight. After about ten minutes, four men from the group mounted and rode north. George realized then that these men did not bring any extra horses. If they made camp, he figured, he may be able to release their horses and scatter them, leaving the group on foot. After what they done, George thought to himself, that's the least that could happen to 'em.

The group did set up camp. It was almost four o'clock and the herd would travel for another three hours or more. George would wait until dark to sneak up and release the group's horses. He once again took the saddle off his horse and used it to lay his head on. He tethered his horse to the ground. As he had another four hours until dark, he closed his eyes and dozed.

When he awoke, he could see the smoke of the group's campfire in the distance. It was nighttime. He sighed, stood, stretched and started the walk towards the group. He circled to the west and there was a slight incline that would help him from being seen. When he was within a half mile of the camp, he hunched down and walked – duck-like – for another quarter mile. He saw how the band of horses was tethered to the ground, some sharing the same stake. All he had to do was pull up all the stakes and scatter the horses. With any luck, the group would be so concerned with getting the horses back they would not notice George at all. George crawled the last quarter mile to where the horses were. He had gone undetected. He got to the first stake, on which three horses were tethered, and pulled it from the ground. He would wait until all the horses were free before spurring them on. He grabbed the second stake with both hands, and pulled it up, freeing two more horses. When he bent down to grab the third stake, he heard the sound of two riders approaching him. "What the hell?" one of the riders shouted.

George yelled for the free horses to scatter, then threw the stake in his hand directly at the closest rider, hitting him in the chest. The second rider pulled out his pistol and aimed it at George. George stepped to the left, drew his hog-leg pistol from its holster and shot the rider in the chest, knocking him completely off his horse. The first rider jumped on George from behind, knocking the pistol out of George's hand. George rolled him over, hit the man's nose with his forehead, and punched the man repeatedly. Blood gushed from the man's nose and mouth. The whole time, the man was cursing George: "You motherless son-of-a-bitch." George heard several gunshots and felt a sharp pain in his right shoulder. Leaving the man under him semi-conscious, he went for the Colt Peacemaker he kept in the back of his belt but his shoulder hurt so much that he could not reach all the way around. Rising to full height, he reached for the pistol with his left hand and fired in the direction of the gunshots. He heard the thud of a body falling and perhaps a second, then several more gunshots. He fell backwards as if pulled from behind. His chest and legs felt as if hot embers had been inserted directly into them. He rolled over on his stomach and tried to stand. He felt more embers enter his buttocks and calves. He fell forward, his face hitting the cold, hard, grassless ground. He tasted the blood in his mouth and, searching with his tongue, felt the empty space where his front teeth had been. He knew he was losing consciousness but also knew he had to fight it. He felt the sensation of a horse landing on his upper back and at the exact same moment heard a loud gunshot, so close it deafened him. That was the last thing George Walsh heard.

Chapter 12

Charlie Smith and Ned Burke had ridden about five miles out of Rio Bravo when they saw two riders approaching them from the direction of the town. Charlie stopped the horses and placed his hand on his pistol. He turned to Burke. "If you so much as open your mouth, I will put a bullet in your other arm."

"Marshall," one of the riders yelled, "Wait up!" Both riders were dressed like ranch hands and when they reached Charlie and Burke, the smell of cattle and horses on them was strong.

"Marshall," the one who had been calling said to Charlie. "Sheriff Chance said you forgot some papers back at the jailhouse." The rider seemed nervous.

Charlie placed a firmer grip on his pistol. "Why didn't you just bring the papers?"

One rider looked at the other. The second one said, "Well, ya see, the Sheriff also needs you to come back to town. He needs help. A gunfight."

Charlie looked at both riders. "'Gunfight?' What kind of gunfight? And just who are you two, anyway?"

The second rider said, "Oh, we deputized. We help out the Sheriff when he needs us."

The first rider nodded, "Yeah, we help him out all the time."

Charlie Smith pulled out his pistol and cocked it before the smile left the face of either rider. "Okay," said Charlie, "Unhook your gun belts and throw 'em on the ground. The same with those rifles."

The first rider began to undo his gun belt. The second hesitated and Charlie pointed the gun at his face. "Son, I will kill you right here. I'm authorized and glad to do it. Now if you don't drop that gun belt on the ground right now, you'll never get a second chance. That's a fact."

Ned Burke threw himself directly at Charlie. Charlie was so big and solid, however, that Burke simply bounced off of him and fell to the ground. The first rider, seeing his chance, reached for his pistol as his unclasped gun belt fell to the ground. He fired and hit Charlie in the stomach. Charlie flinched but shot the rider through the head. The second rider reached for his rifle and jumped off his horse. While he cocked the trigger of the Scofield, Charlie shot him twice in the chest. The second rider collapsed to the ground.

Burke tried to stand but between the handcuffs and bad arm, he could only get to his knees. "I think you broke my other arm, you fat bastard!" he yelled at Charlie.

Charlie looked down at the blood coming from his stomach wound and wiped at it as if it was merely mud on his shirt. Without looking at Burke, he yelled back, "Oh, shut the hell up you little squint or I'll cripple ya."

Charlie got off his horse and looked at the two dead bodies. He picked one up, put him over his shoulder and reached for the reins of the man's horse. The other dead man's horse had run away after his owner had fallen from it. Charlie put the man's body across the saddle. He picked up the other man and draped him next to the first one. He then grabbed Burke by the shoulder and lifted him half off the ground. He carried him to the horse Dude had provided him and placed Burke's foot in the stirrup.

"Where we goin'?" Burke demanded. "You gotta take me back to Rio Bravo. The doc's gotta look at my other arm. And you can't make it to Laredo, you'll bleed to death."

Charlie looked up at Burke, "One more word. One more word and I will tie you to the back of this horse and let him drag you from here on. I swear to God Almighty."

Charlie felt slightly dizzy. He grabbed the kerchief from the neck of one of the dead men and used it to stop the blood coming from his stomach. "Damn," he said. He got up on his horse, grabbed the reins from Burke's horse, went to the horse with the two dead men, and headed back to Rio Bravo.

Chapter 13

For Nathan Burdette's new saloon, Rudolph Trenton had a bar built and shipped from carpenters he knew in St. Louis. He got a piano in from Denver and hired a piano player from Fort Worth. He brought in two pool tables made by the A.E. Schmidt Billiard Company in St. Louis. Trenton also hired experienced faro and blackjack dealers from around the Southwest. For the opening night, Nathan Burdette had hired a Mexican band that performed such tunes as "Cielito Lindo", "La Sandunga", and "Bella Rosa" from a large stage designed by Trenton. Trenton had also brought in a dozen sporting ladies, planning on making half of them permanent.

The opening night of Burdette's saloon was attended by local and out-of-town patrons. Burdette was trying to create a Texas cattlemen association and invited some of the largest ranchers throughout the state. Maggie was dressed in a blue flowing gown she said was shipped from Europe. She also wore fishnet stockings and high-button blue shoes she had ordered from "back East." She moved among the crowd as if she was the party's hostess.

Dude was doing his rounds when the guests started to arrive at the saloon. While he had promised Chance he would avoid the saloon that night, he could not overcome the feeling that he had to see Maggie before the evening started. He felt he had to remind her that he was here, that he loved her. He deliberately slowed his pace as he passed the Burdette saloon. A banner announcing "Grand Opening" in red and blue lettering was draped over the second story.

Trenton noticed him first and went outside to greet him. "Deputy," he said, "You will be joining us tonight, won't you?"

Dude stopped. "Well," he began, "officially, I'm on duty."

Trenton replied, "Wait right here. I'll get Maggie. Maybe she can persuade you."

After a minute or two, Maggie came out with Trenton. Trenton made a slight bow to her and Dude and went back inside. Maggie said, "What is this about you being on duty, 'officially'? Are you coming to this party or not?"

Dude felt compelled to walk right up to her. He bent in to kiss her on the lips but she turned her head to the side. "No, not now," she whispered, "*I* am on duty. Officially."

Dude turned away in frustration. "What if I asked you not to go? You and me can go riding out to the Grande. Make a picnic." He turned back to her.

She smiled and said, "We talked about this. This is business and I have to tend to business. You can come up afterward. For pleasure." She touched his cheek, turned, and went back inside the saloon.

Dude watched her after she went back inside. He saw her walk up to a man in a suit, tie, and checkered vest. He had seen the man before. Dude had seen him in the small Laredo courthouse when Dude had to testify against the Bolan brothers a few months back. The man was a lawyer, perhaps Burdette's lawyer. Dude watched as Maggie laughed with the man and patted his arm. A voice inside Dude's head told him that he had seen enough and that he had to complete his rounds. He turned and headed back towards the jailhouse. On the way, he passed the old saloon, the Long Branch. He stopped and went in. The bar was comprised of wide maple planks across oak barrels. He walked up to it and kidded the bartender, "I bet you ain't expecting many customers tonight, eh, Dave?"

"Well," replied Dave, "I ain't worried. They'll come back when they either run out of money or the shine on Burdette's place starts to fade. Wanna beer?"

Dude scratched his chin. "What's that stuff Stumpy drinks?"

Dave was surprised. "Whiskey? You, Dude? That'll be a first. Yeah, Stumpy drinks Irish whiskey. I always keep a few bottles in stock. It's smoother than most. Want I should pour you a shot?"

Dude didn't reply at first. He thought about the empty feeling Stumpy had described. He felt, or at least thought he felt, that emptiness. "Sure, Dave," he finally said, "lemme try it."

Dude was expecting the burn but it did not come. Dave was right: it was smooth. Certainly less harsh than the one or two drinks of rotgut he had had in the past. "Hey, Dave, give me another."

Dave obliged but cautioned, "That's strong stuff, Dude. Better respect it, especially that you're not used to it."

Dude drank the second shot. It's just liquid, he thought to himself. It's not flesh and blood of someone punching me or taking shots at me. Surely, that's tougher. And I always won those battles. This is a reward for winning those. This is for me. I deserve this. Nothing can beat me. Not bullets. Not fists. Not even women. A woman. He reached into his pocket, pulled out two silver dollars, and placed them on the bar. "Hey, Dave," he said out loud, "Can you spare a bottle of this?"

Dave had been a bartender most of his adult life. He had witnessed the pleasure and good times that liquor brings as well as the pain and hurt. He liked Dude and admired him. Dude had lawman skills but was also fair and kind. He saw Dude break up fights in this very place without using his fists or a gun. Dude always seemed in control so why wouldn't he be in control now? Dave reached down, placed a new bottle of Irish whiskey on the bar in front of Dude, and took the two dollars.

Dude took the bottle and the glass in front of him and thanked Dave. He walked over to an empty table; as they were all empty, he had his choice. He broke the seal of the bottle and poured a shot. He drank that and poured another. "I'm just doing what they're all doing," Dude thought to himself. "This is what it's like to be normal. Not having to worry about being the best at something, about doing the right thing all the time. I'm complete now. I'm even more complete than them. This will make me be like them, just more so. This must be why they do it. To make themselves stop hurting." He poured another and felt the image of Maggie as his woman begin to materialize. He closed his eyes and forced the image away until it dissolved. He drank and then poured another. Stumpy was right: drink it for the taste.

Chapter 14

Nine men stood over George Walsh's lifeless body. Two of the men were holding torches. "Yeah, he's one a'them," one man said.

A second man said, "That tears it! This is horseshit! I say we just attack and kill 'em all and take that goddamn herd. We out-number 'em, we got more guns. Let's finish it."

"That ain't the way Burdette wants it," said another of the men, whose tone implied that he was in charge.

The man responded, "Well, Burdette ain't out here playin' Indjun and getting killed! We lost Billy, Big Mike, Red, and Lucas's head probably busted. We're also down a half dozen horses thanks to this son-of-a-bitch. Let's rush 'em and get it over with."

The man in charge said, "That ain't the plan, Curtis!"

"The plan ain't working, Chris," said Curtis. "Them drovers haven't turned tail and left the herd. They just keep goin'. And the farther north they go the longer it'll take us to get that herd down to Mexico. Besides, Billy and Red were the best with the bow and arrow."

Chris said calmly, "The plan isn't to kill them all. At least one's gotta get back to say they was attacked by Comanch' or Kiowa."

Curtis shot back, "Well this guy don't look like he was killed by no Kiowa. What Kiowas you know use buckshot?"

Chris thought for a moment. "We can still scare 'em off. Or bargain with 'em."

"'Bargain with 'em'?" said Curtis. "With what? Let the herd go and we won't kill ya? Then they go back and say that white men stole the herd. That don't cut it. Ya just said so yaself."

"Okay, then," said Chris, "we scare 'em. Who's got a knife?" One of the men handed Chris a large hunting knife. Chris knelt down and started to cut George's scalp, just under the hairline from the forehead to the middle of George's head. Two of the men standing, turned their backs and another began to vomit. Chris stood up, holding the knife in one bloody hand, George's scalp in the other. "Okay," he said to the assembled group, "strip him, find something that will identify him – like his bandana. Get his horse, too. In the morning we ride ahead, put an arrow through this," he indicated the scalp, "and the bandana, up ahead where they'll find it. They'll think it was Kiowas then and they'll run. Let's get a meeting going now. And I'll need two volunteers to run ahead first thing tomorrow."

Four of the men bent over George's body and began to cut away his clothes, pull off his boots, and go through his possessions. One man, shoving George's bills into his own pocket came across George's Texas Ranger badge. "Jesus," said the man, "this guy was a Ranger," and showed the badge to Chris. "You think they all Rangers?"

Chris looked at the badge in his hand. "Nah. Why would Texas Rangers be punchin' cows? But this is it," he said handing the badge back. "Put this with the arrow and the scalp."

Once George Walsh's body was rendered completely naked, the men walked back to the campfire and joined the rest of the group.

Chapter 15

When Charlie Smith came riding into the city limits of Rio Bravo, leading Ned Burke and the horse with two dead bodies, he was fighting consciousness. The first person to notice him was Tommy Baylor, a young boy who cleaned out the Gibbs stables. Tommy was wiping down some of the horses before going in to eat his supper when his saw Charlie and the two horses. Tommy had seen Charlie with Sheriff Chance earlier that day and was amazed at Charlie's size. He knew he was a lawman and ran to the jailhouse to get Chance.

In the jailhouse, Chance told Tommy to get Doc Fix and then to find Dude. He grabbed his Winchester rifle and ran down to get Charlie and to put Edwards back in the cell. He took the reins of the other two horses out of Charlie's hand and led both horses to a hitching post. Chance then helped Charlie get down off his horse and let him lean on him as they walked down the street towards Doc Fix's office. "Hey," yelled Burke, "what about me? My arm's broke!"

Chance did not respond. He continued to support Charlie as they walked down the street. Burke continued to yell after them.

#

Doc Fix's office was a converted front bedroom in the clapboard house he built when he and his wife first settled in Rio Bravo. He cleared his examination table and helped Chance place Charlie on it. "Belly," whispered Charlie.

Doc Fix cut away Charlie's shirt and examined the wound. "It ain't deep, mister, but you lost a lot of blood." He turned to Chance, "He should be okay as long as there's no infection. Funny, I was just reading about blood transfusions for humans. I don't have the equipment and it's risky, but this would be a perfect case for it." He turned back to Charlie, "It's a good thing you're so strong 'cause that's what saved you really. Now I have to take this bullet out. It'll hurt – maybe not as much as when you were shot – but the pain will ease right after. I'll stitch you up then you get some rest. We'll get a couple of big steaks in you, and you'll be fine."

Chance left the doctor's house and headed back to Burke and the two dead bodies. Burke was still yelling. "My ass hurts! Get me down from here!" As Chance approached the horse with the two dead men, and without responding or looking at Burke, he pushed him and Burke fell the to the ground. Chance then picked up the head of each of the dead men. He did not recognize either. Tommy Baylor came running up to him.

"Find Dude?" Chance asked.

"No sir," said Tommy. He ain't in his hotel room either."

"Probably with that woman," Chance muttered to himself. To Tommy, he said, "Here's five dollars, go to Bert the mortician, give him that and tell him we got two for him." Chance took out a silver dollar. "And this is for you, Tommy. Thanks."

Tommy thanked Chance and ran to the funeral parlor to find Bert. Chance picked Burke off the ground and headed toward the jailhouse. He finally addressed Burke directly, "You see either of those men before?"

Burke spat on the ground, "Never. Don't know them from Adam. When's the Doc gonna see me about my arm. And I think you broke my back."

Chance did not say another word to Burke for the rest of the walk. When they reached the jailhouse, he uncuffed Burke and placed him in the same cell that Burke had been in for the past two weeks. "Get the Doc," yelled Burke,

"He's busy," said Chance as he slammed the cell door.

Chapter 16

It was daybreak and Diego was using the extra morning coffee to extinguish the fire. Joe approached him. "Hold up," he said, "Let me get one last one," as he stuck out his cup. Diego poured the coffee then continued to put out the fire. Ted approached the two men.

"George ever show up last night?" he asked Joe.

Joe drank from his coffee cup before saying, "No, and I didn't sleep. I thought every breeze and every damn coyot' was him. He said if they wasn't the men, he'd let 'em go and be back. Shit." He threw the rest of the coffee on the ground. "Let's just keep movin' with the same set-up as yesterday. Take point." He went to his horse, mounted and rode to the herd. "Okay, let's get 'em up and movin!" And the drive continued.

It was right before noon when Ted, searching for grazing land for the next break, saw the body of the dead coyote in the distance. Just like with Harper Turner's body, the arrow served as a marker. Ted took out his pistol, looked in all directions, and rode out to the body of the dead animal. He dismounted, squatted within arm's length and examined it. After a few moments, he got on his horse and rode back to the herd. He galloped past Bradford Beaverson on the right front part of the herd and rode right up to Joe Edwards.

"What is it, Ted?" asked Joe, "Find grazin'?"

Ted was breathing hard from the ride. "Can ya stop 'em here? I need ya to come up with me," he said, between breaths.

Joe nodded and turned to Pete behind him. He waved his arm and yelled, "Stop 'em here!" He rode with Ted and when he passed Bradford said, "Stoppin' 'em here, Brad. You get the boys to take a break and switch horses." Bradford nodded in response.

When Joe and Ted came to the dead coyote, they both dismounted. Ted pointed at the arrow with the toe of his boot and said, "Look." At the entry point of the arrow, there was a matted piece of what looked like an additional patch of fur hard with dried blood. Tied to the arrow's shaft was George Walsh's Texas Ranger badge.

Joe said to no one, "My God." He looked at Ted, "And I'm guessing that's right through its heart?" He forced himself to touch the feathers of the arrow sticking out of the coyote's ribcage.

Ted shook his head. He placed his foot underneath the animal's back and rolled it over, revealing a bullet hole in the coyote's head. "I ain't as good as George about these things, naturally, but I don't think Comanch' or Kiowa kill this way. One arrow would do it. I think this is white men. Judgin' by the hole, I'd say it was from a small gun, a Peacemaker maybe – a repeater. And this didn't happen long ago: no flies yet, no signs of decay. They're close by, Joe."

Joe stared at the body for a minute, thinking about what George had told him about Indians attacking on horseback and not leaving dead steer to rot. "Well," he said finally, "Let's go back and talk to the boys. See if they want to go on or not." He rolled the coyote over with his foot, bent down and untied George Walsh's badge from the arrow. He took a bandana from his back pocket and rolled the badge in it. He placed the bandana in his shirt pocket. He got on his horse and, with Ted, rode back to the herd.

The herd was grazing and Bradford Beaverson and Burny Palmer were slowly circling it, making soothing, calming sounds. Every once in a while, Burny would softly sing or hum a song. Joe and Ted rode past Burny and they each provided an acknowledging wave, the two then rode directly to the wagon. Diego was helping Pete saddle his fresh horse. Burtrum Hayes was drinking water from one of the barrels in the wagon. Joe dismounted, looked briefly at Ted, and walked up to Burtrum, who nodded at Joe. Joe rubbed his chin, grabbed a tin cup and filled it with water from the barrel. "Pete, Diego, please come here," he said.

Burtrum, Pete and Diego faced Joe while Ted stayed in his saddle. Joe drained the contents of his cup, and said, "Ted found this," then he unwrapped George Walsh's badge, "along with his scalp."

"Mother of God," said Burtrum.

Pete and Diego both made the sign of the cross and whispered, "Dios mio."

Joe continued, "That's not all. George suspected, and me and Ted agree, that it's white men doing this."

Burtrum was perplexed, "Why would white men scalp? And all them blasted arrows?"

Joe hesitated and looked into the distance. "Maybe to spook us, scare us off, then take the herd."

Burtrum shook his head and replied, "Sorry to say this, Joe, but it's working. I've been so nervous I can't sleep or shit. Now this…"

"Well," said Joe, "and this goes for you too, Pete and Diego, I leave it to you to decide if you want to go on. As for me, I'm with this herd like I'm sewed to it." He looked up at Ted, "Sorry, Ted, didn't mean to leave you out. But if you want to leave, I understand. I can just about pay you your wages up to now."

Diego shook his head, "No, I work for Stumpy and the job he give me now is this herd. And can you drive a wagon and herd cows at the same time, Joe? I don't think so."

Joe smiled at Diego and nodded. "Yeah," he said, "I don't think so either. Thank you, Diego."

Burtrum spoke next. "Me and Harper rode together on and off for eighteen years. He'd look down and think I was one sorry son-of-a-bitch if I gave up after all what happened. Besides, I can sleep and shit when we get to Colorado."

Joe laughed out loud and said, "Thank you, Burt."

Pete looked at Joe and said, "You're short-handed as it is. If any of us quit it'd be like giving up the herd anyway, so count me in."

Joe nodded and said, "Gracias, amigo." Then he looked up at Ted, "Well, Pinkerton Man, what do you say?"

Ted sighed and said, "Joe, after seein' what I just seen, I'm more mad than scared. Call me insane but I want to run into these bastards. Right now I wanna kill every last one of 'em." He turned his horse around and headed towards the herd.

Joe placed his cup back in the wagon and mounted his horse. "Thanks, men. I got two more hands I gotta ask," and rode out to the herd.

He approached Bradford first. "Brad," he began, "Ted found something up ahead. Whoever's been following' likely killed George last night. Your mother's already lost one son on this drive and I don't want her to lose another. I can pay you your wages and we can plan out a safe route back to home for you."

Bradford face reddened, "Joe, I'm as good a hand now as any of the others. You need me. You can't get this herd through with only – what – six men and a wagon! We'll make it there and back. I know it. Please don't send me home. If I go it's like Taylor died for nothin'. Please, Joe."

Joe looked down at his saddle horn and was quiet for a while. "Okay," he said looking up at Bradford, "But you stay close to me, Brad. Keep me in your sight and I'll try to do the same with you. I ain't never met your mom but she should be right proud of you. And your brother." He rode on to Burny.

Burny was finishing one of the two verses he knew of "Buffalo Gal" when Joe rode up. He smiled at Joe. "We movin' 'em on again, Joe?"

Joe fidgeted in his saddle. "Burny," he said, "I know you signed on as a favor to Stumpy but this is turnin' out to be more than a drive. Ted found George's badge up ahead. Whoever attacked us probably killed him last night. It's probably white men, not Indians. It's likely we're gonna run into them again. You can leave if you want and I – and the rest of us – will still think you are one of the best and bravest men we ever rode with."

Burny smiled broadly. "Brave? I ain't brave enough to face my Ma and tell her I let Stumpy down. I think I'd rather have white men or Indians or – hell, bears – kill me first than tell her I failed a friend of hers. No, sir, y'all are stuck with me until we finish this thing." He smiled again at Joe.

Joe smiled back and said, "Well, sir, you are all either the toughest or craziest bunch I ever come across. Either way, I'm proud to be riding with ya. I swear to God, I am." He reached out his hand and shook Burny's. He then turned around to reorganize the drive.

Chapter 17

Dude awoke outside the back wall of Gibbs' stables. He had dried vomit on his shirt and his head ached. Next to his arm was the half-empty bottle of Irish whiskey. He sat up and tried to collect his thoughts. The stable? The stable? Yes, that's right. He was going to saddle up Maggie's horse and take her away. But he had felt so tired he thought he would lay down first.

The sun shone so bright over the roof of the stable that Dude had to close his eyes. Judging by the position of that sun, it must have been mid-morning. He rose to stand but his head hurt even more. I should check in with Chance, he thought. Dude redoubled his effort to stand and right himself. He leaned on the stable wall to get his balance and then slowly walked towards the jailhouse. He saw Doc Fix's carriage parked outside of it. He walked in and found the doctor examining Ned Burke in the same cell the criminal had occupied for two weeks. Dude wiped his mouth. Was it a dream that Charlie Smith had taken Burke to Laredo, he thought at first. What did that stuff do to him, he wondered. Gaining clarity, he said, "What the hell is Burke doin' back here again?"

Chance walked in from the back of the jailhouse. "Just where the hell have you been? Look at yourself. Smell yourself!"

Dude immediately became self-conscious and looked down at the dried vomit on his shirt and vest. "I got sick," was all he could manage.

Chance replied, "While you were off being 'sick' two men shot Charlie. He'll be alright and he got both of them. I think they may have worked for Nathan Burdette. You've been out to the Burdette ranch lately, maybe you can identify them. This is what I need you to do: first, get yourself cleaned up; then go over to Bert's and look over the bodies. Come back and tell me if you've seen them before."

Dude turned to leave.

Chance said, "Dude, whatever happened to you last night, don't let it happen again."

Embarrassed, Dude left.

Doc Fix walked out of Burke's cell. Chance closed the door behind him. Fix said, "Oh, he's fine other than opening the stitches I put in him last time. Nothing broken. I sewed him up a bit."

Chance nodded and said, "How's Charlie?"

Fix smiled. "Well, he's weak but weak for him is strong for any other man. Say, where did you two meet anyway?"

Chance smiled and said, "In the calvary. Charlie was one of my corporals. We've been through some times him and me."

Fix whistled. "Between the two of you it's a wonder them Comanches didn't just take one look and surrender." Both men laughed.

Just as Doc Fix was leaving the jailhouse, four men rode up. They each got off their horse and went in.

"Hey, Sheriff," one man demanded. "We hear you're holdin' a man what tried to kill a U.S. Marshall." The other three men gathered behind him. "We think a man like that should be hung. This town don't feel good about anybody that tries to kill someone who supposed to protect them. Whether he succeeds or not. We'd feel the same way if someone tried to kill you, Sheriff."

Chance stared at the man. "Well, I'm deeply touched," he said. "But first of all, when did the town elect you their spokesman? Especially since I've never seen you in this town before. Secondly, you don't have the facts. You're like a bunch of old biddies going off half-cocked with gossip. And last," he said as he took his saddle-ring Winchester rifle out of the rack behind him, "get out." He cocked the rifle. "Get out and don't come back."

The man backed away and weakly put up his hands. "Sheriff, you don't understand. This is what the townspeople want and it's for your own good."

Chance stared at the man and then looked at the three men behind him. "If I see any of you back here, I'll either arrest you." He paused, "Or kill you."

The men walked out. Once on their horses, the man who did all the talking said to Chance, "You ain't heard the last of this, Sheriff. You're makin' a mistake!" The men rode off. Chance stood in the doorway and watched them as they left. He went back in the jailhouse and placed a chair directly in front of Burke's cell. "Ned," he began, "If I'm right, I believe Nathan Burdette wants you dead. Those two dead men who you didn't know from Adam weren't sent to rescue you. They were sent to kill you. If you got something on Burdette, now would be a good time to tell me. I think those men – and probably more – are coming back. I've seen this before: get a whole town riled up over nothing. Or to do a single man's bidding. You can save both of us a lot of trouble if you just tell me what Burdette hired you for."

Ned Burke used his good arm to rub the top of his head. "You ain't gonna let 'em lynch me, are ya, Sheriff? Ya can't! You ain't allowed to! You supposed to protect me. I got rights!"

Chance looked down. "I'll do what I can but it'll help us both if you told me about any deal you had with Burdette."

Just then, Dude walked into the jailhouse. He was wearing a new shirt and pants and smelled clean. "John T.," he said, "one of those men was Willie Hawkins, he just started working for Burdette. He was mean. Not too smart but real mean."

Chance said, "That's what I thought. Burdette's also trying to get folks riled up to lynch Burke. We gotta stop that."

Dude smiled. "Lynching Burke ain't such a bad idea. Maybe I'll join 'em."

Chance stared at Dude, "That's not funny Dude. He may be the only thing we got to connecting Burdette to something bigger. Now that I think of it, a lot of the things you've been doing lately aren't particularly funny."

Dude rubbed his face and said, "Yeah, just letting off some steam, I guess. I got it under control."

Chance left it at that. "Good," he said. "Now stay with Burke and I'll go see how Charlie's doing. Carlos gave him the back room of the hotel."

Dude smiled and said, "Sure. I'll stay with Burke. Punishment enough."

Chance went over to the hotel. He passed the Long Branch Saloon and saw a crowd at the bar. "Burdette wouldn't want that sort of thing going on at his own place and splash back on him," he thought to himself.

#

Charlie was sitting up in bed as Chance walked in the door. "How ya feeling, Charlie," he said.

Charlie grinned and said, "Oh, like a darn fool, John. Those two idiots came up and I should have scared 'em away right off. I shouldn'ta killed them. And Dude's right: that Burke is a shitheel."

Chance sat in the chair next to the bed. "Anybody you want me to contact back home?" he said.

Charlie thought for a moment. "A wire to my wife would be good, John. Much appreciated. Maybe send it to the courthouse. She'll get it."

Chance nodded. "I'll do that straight away. We think those two men worked for Nathan Burdette, a local rancher who seems to want to own the whole territory. I'm thinking they came to kill Burke. Did they say anything?"

Charlie shook his head. "No, just some stupid lies about you forgetting to give me some papers and that they were deputized by you. When you told me Dude was the only one you needed, I knew they were full of horseshit. Doc says I'll be up and around in a couple of days but the ride back home will have to wait a week while these stiches heal. That Pedro fella is really good. It's as if he and his wife can't do enough for me."

Chance smiled and nodded his head. "Yeah, they're good people. You keep resting and I'll get that wire out to your wife." Chance left the hotel and headed towards the telegraph office.

Chapter 18

The herd was about twenty-five miles outside of Texline, Oklahoma. Pete Gomez was on point while Ted Davis took over Pete's wing position on the upper right side of the herd. Bradford Beaverson was now opposite him on the left. Joe was behind Bradford, and Burny Palmer was behind Joe. Behind Ted on the right was Burtrum Hayes who was responsible for the largest section of the herd, actually covering two positions. Between Ted and Burtrum were Diego and the wagon.

#

Two miles east of the herd was the group that had been following it for the last five hundred miles. Chris, the leader of the group, rode ahead of the nineteen remaining men. Some of them had doubled up on horses. George Walsh's horse was being ridden by two men. Among the ones sharing a horse was a man with a bandaged head, the bandage comprised of a leg from a cut-up longjohn. Both of the man's eyes were blackened and his nose was broken and swollen. The man named Curtis rode up to Chris.

"What're thinkin' of doin', Chris?" said Curtis. "We're runnin' out of time."

"I know that, damnit," said Chris. "The scalp didn't spook 'em and we got no cover least I can see. I'm thinking on payin' them a visit tonight. Surround them. Bows and arrows. Pick 'em off. If that ain't workin', maybe make a deal. Tell 'em none of 'em can go back to Rio Bravo, at least not for a while. If that don't work, we gotta kill 'em. We outnumber them more than three-to-one from what I figure." Chris used the spyglass that belonged to George Walsh and looked in the direction of the herd. "We keep pace with 'em until tonight, then close in and surround them."

#

Bradford Beaverson was falling asleep in his saddle again. Burtrum had told him it was okay and an old cowhand trick. But when Bradford realized he had dozed off he cursed himself for not being fully attentive of all the new dangers around him. He grabbed his canteen, poured water into his hand and splashed it on his face. Stay awake, he said to himself, stay awake. It seemed to him that Burtrum, Burny and Joe didn't need sleep. He wanted to be like that. But he was relieved when he saw the sun begin to set because he knew the herd would be stopped soon. That meant coffee, food, and some sleep.

Pete found a good place to stop the cattle and the cowhands gathered in the herd and then began to make camp. Joe said he would take the first watch and that Ted could relieve him. As usual, Burny would take the last shift, humming and singing to the cows until daybreak.

As he unsaddled his horse, Burny yelled over to Diego, "How about a couple of them chickens tonight?"

Diego smiled and nodded, grabbed two chickens from the crate in the back of the wagon and started to prepare them for dinner.

Bradford dropped his saddle across from the fire that Burtrum had just started. He lay down and placed his head on it and closed his eyes. He fell asleep almost immediately. Pete dropped his saddle a few feet away from Bradford's. He placed his rifle across the seat. Since George Walsh's killing, all the hands, except for Bradford, slept with their rifles close by.

Joe came riding in from his watch. His took off his horse's saddle and joined the others by the fire, placing himself next to Bradford. He poured some coffee and took a piece of chicken from the pan Diego had left out. He sat back to eat. Bradford and Pete were asleep. Burtrum and Burny were on the other side of the fire from Joe, talking softly. An arrow fell directly into the fire. Throwing aside his cup and plate, Joe picked up his carbine rifle and cocked it. Burtrum and Burny, wide-eyed, each grabbed their rifles and crawled in the direction from which the arrow came. Joe poked Bradford with the butt of his rifle and put up his hand to tell him to be quiet. Burtrum roused Pete, then turned to Joe and mouthed, "The herd. Ted," then, staying low, ran towards the herd.

A second arrow overshot the fire and landed two feet past Burny's saddle. A third fell harmlessly, yards from the wagon. Joe was afraid of this situation. A single shot could spook the cattle and he would have another stampede to deal with, this time in the dark. He looked at the anxious faces around him. He closed his eyes and took a deep breath before calling out into the dark, "We know you ain't Kiowa or Comanch'! We know you ain't savages! Come out and show yourselves like civilized men!" He lay completely still, silently praying his gamble would pay off.

#

Near the herd, Ted was slowly riding around the cattle. By his estimate, this would be the third complete circle he had made that night. Burtrum was on the opposite side of the herd and quietly called Ted's name. He began to move to his left, crouching and looking for Ted. The moon provided the only light and Burtrum used the cattle to feel his way around. He stopped and thought of going the other way, hoping to find Ted coming towards him. He turned to his right and saw a smiling face in front of him. Seeing the face confused him for just an instant and he stopped. He felt a sharp pain in his stomach as the man shoved a knife just above Burtrum's gun belt. Burtrum dropped his rifle and grabbed at his belly, feeling the warm blood pouring from it. The fingers of Burtrum's right hand got in the way of the knife as the man pulled it out of Burtrum's stomach. Burtrum's index and middle fingers were sliced off. As he looked down at his belly and missing fingers, he felt a hand violently cover his face and his head was pulled back as a second man cut his throat. Burtrum Hayes fell to his knees, slumped over to the ground and died.

The two men wiped their knives on Burtrum's shirt and one picked up his rifle as the other undid Burtrum's gun belt and carried it off to rejoin their group. When they got back there, Chris and Curtis were arguing via whispers.

"They know we ain't Injuns," said Curtis. "Let's just rush 'em! Now!"

"Let me think, goddamnit, let me think!" said Chris. He looked up and saw Burtrum Hayes' killers. They each nodded to Chris and he said, "Good." He looked at Curtis and whispered, "They's one man down. Another one."

Curtis looked at the two killers, then back to Chris. "That leaves them five, I think. These odds are getting better all the time. We gotta attack!"

#

Ted Davis thought he had heard something or someone move in the distance and figured it was Burny coming to relieve him. I think he's a bit early, he thought to himself, but I'm not going to argue; I could use the rest. He then heard the distinct sound of an arrow whizzing by him, about three feet to his left. He heard someone utter, "Shit!" Ted jumped from his horse and grabbed his Scofield rifle out of its scabbard. He held the rifle backwards, with his right hand on the barrel and his left on the stock. He ran, crouching, towards the sound of the voice and came upon a bearded man fumbling with a bow and arrow. Ted hit the man in the forehead with the butt of his rifle and when the man's head jerk back, he hit him again, harder, directly in the man's throat. The man fell down on his back. Ted then took the opportunity to grind his boot heel into the man's crotch. Since the man's larynx was completely shattered, he could not scream out. Ted continued to step on the man's scrotum, imagining he was planting it in the ground like pieces of potato. Then he heard someone running away from him and he dropped his rifle and immediately gave chase. In the moonlight, he saw a figure two yards in front of him. He dived forward and caught the running man by the legs. Ted took out his knife and climbed on top of the man. The man grabbed Ted's right wrist with his left hand and Ted held the man's right wrist with his own left hand. The man knew he was overpowered and Ted saw that knowledge in the man's eyes.

"Please," the man said, "Mister! No, please!"

Ted became incensed. "'Please?'" he whispered violently. "Did my friend say 'please' when you goddamned jackals were scalping him?" He raised his right hand up, out of the man's grip and then grabbed the man's left wrist with his left hand and used his left forearm to pin both of arms to the man's sides. Then Ted used all his might to stab the man though his breastplate and plunged the knife into the man's heart. The man jerked his head back and started to scream but Ted used his left hand to cover the man's mouth. Ted placed his shoulder on the back of the knife and pushed the blade into the man's chest up to the handle. The man squirmed the entire time and then began to shake violently. He could no longer scream and Ted placed both of his hands on the handle of the knife and moved the blade up and down and side to side. When the man was completely still, Ted rolled off him and took the knife out of the man's chest, having to use both of his hands. He wiped the blade on his own pants and stood up. He found a bow by the man's head and picked it up. He kicked the man's dead body over and grabbed the remaining arrows in the quiver strung across the man's back. Ted's hands were shaking fiercely and the man's blood was spilling from them in all directions. He closed his eyes and took a deep breath. A bow and arrow, he thought to himself, what the hell do I know about using a bow and arrow?

#

Chris decided to surround the camp before responding to Joe's call. He sent the two men who had killed Burtrum Hayes along with four others in the direction of the herd with instructions to loop quietly around the camp. Once there, they were to light an arrow and fire it into the air. The six men headed out. The man who had stabbed Burtrum was the first to discover the body of the man Ted Davis had stabbed in the heart. "Christ on a cross," he said, "Who coulda done this?" The other men looked around in all directions. Just then, an arrow struck one of the men in the head, glancing off his skull and knocking his hat off. A second arrow struck the man in his left shoulder. A third missed the man completely. The five uninjured men squatted down and looked in the direction of the arrow. Almost fifteen seconds had passed when another arrow struck the man – the same man who had slit Burtrum Hayes' throat – in the back.

#

Seeing the arrow in the man's back, Ted Davis silently congratulated himself on getting the knack of the bow-and-arrow. Unfortunately, he had just shot the last arrow that he had found in the dead man's quiver. Placing the bow quietly on the ground, he started to pick up rocks, each the size of a duck egg, and placed them in the nook of his left arm. Then he started to toss them, one at a time and as hard as he could, in the direction of the group of men. One rock hit a man directly in the left eye and another hit a man in his jaw, cracking all the teeth on the left side of the man's mouth.

Getting impatient that he had not seen the flaming arrow yet, Chris sent two more men in the direction of the herd. After walking about fifty yards, the two came upon a man throwing rocks, about twenty more yards ahead of them. One man turned to the other and put his finger to his lips. He then took out a long knife from the sheath attached to his belt and held it by the blade. He then crept up behind the rock thrower. When he was within five yards, he threw the knife, hitting Ted in the right kidney. Ted fell to his knees. The knifer-thrower then ran up to Ted, grabbed the rock Ted was about to throw, and brought it down on his head. He hit Ted four more times with the rock. The man then took his knife out of Ted's back and cut the ex-Pinkerton Detective's throat. Ted Davis died under the glow of the Oklahoma moonlight.

The man removed his knife from Ted Davis' back and wiped it on the back of Ted's leather vest. He then motioned for the other man to join him and they proceeded to go in the direction of the herd. They came upon the group that was sent ahead of them. One man had his hand to his eye, blood dripping between his fingers. Another was holding his mouth, crying in pain. "Shut up, ya little baby!" said one of the men. "And let's keep going." The man with the arrow in his back, the same man who had murdered Burtrum Hayes, had passed out due to the loss of blood and the others walked around him. The one with the arrow in his shoulder was being catered to by another man, who told him the arrow was not in too deep. He wrapped a bandana around the puncture and told the wounded man that it would best to take the arrow out once they had light and hot water.

Using the cowhand's fire as a focal point, the group stopped once they agreed they were directly on the other side. The man who had stabbed Burtrum Hayes earlier in the night took the bow and an arrow from the man with the broken jaw. He pointed the tip of the arrow towards another man and told him to light it. Being careful not to accidently touch the flame, he fired the arrow into the air behind the group.

Chris saw the flame and stood up. "Hey, in the camp," he called, "we're coming in." Chris waved his hand and the remaining men followed him forward.

Seeing the flaming arrow and then hearing the shout, Joe Edwards immediately knew the two actions were associated and realized he had let himself get surrounded. He stood up, his rifle in hand and faced Chris and the oncoming group. Burny Palmer and Pete Gomez, sitting next to each other and facing the rear of their camp saw the other group approach. It was a strange sight: one man had an arrow in his shoulder, was hatless and had blood dripping from his head; another was holding a blood-soaked rag to his eye; and another had both hands on his jaw, moaning in pain. On either side of that group was a man holding a bow and arrow, aiming it at the cowhands.

Chris' group had four men with bows and arrows, also at the ready and pointed at various cowhands. The young Mexican man pointing his arrow at Burny Palmer was visibly scared and his hands were shaking.

Joe looked at Chris and said, "Chris Lomax. I knew Burdette had a hand in this."

Chris smiled and replied, "You might as well put down that rifle, Joe. And that goes for all you others. We all know you ain't about to fire and start a stampede."

Joe breathed a heavy sigh but kept his rifle. Chris looked at him and said, "Joe, it didn't have to be like this. You shoulda taken the job Burdette offered you, or just rode off. But no, you did neither. 'Cause you stubborn. Stubborn like a woman or a spoiled child. And look what happened. Good men were killed on both sides."

Joe shook his head, and replied, "No, just on one side."

Chris smiled again and said, "Be that as it may, as my own mother used to say to me. But was it worth it, Joe?"

Joe said, "I understand it all now: this drive fails and Burdette makes a play for Stumpy's land."

Chris looked at Joe and said, "Yeah, somethin' like that. People like you and Stumpy don't see it. Nathan Burdette is a great man. He's a man with vision. He sees growth and prosperity for the whole region, not just for himself. People like you and Stumpy don't understand progress. You might as well be put on the reservation ya'selves."

Joe sighed and said, "Okay, just take the herd and go. Let these men be."

Chris laughed, "Oh, you know I can't do that. No one can go back to Rio Bravo and tell what really happened out here. This was a Kiowa attack. Or Comanch'. It don't really matter."

Burny Palmer stood up and said, "Then let the boy go, at least," and pointed at Bradford Beaverson.

Chris looked at Bradford and said, "You look familiar, boy. Ain't you from around Rio Bravo?"

Bradford nervously looked at Joe who shook his head subtly.

"I bet you wanna go home, doncha, son?" Chris continued, "Home to you mama."

Joe searched Chris's face for any signs that he would give some type of order to hurt Brad. Just then, the nervous youth who was pointing his bow and arrow at Burny let the arrow fly. It struck Burny right in the sternum. Because the distance was so close, the arrow went almost completely through Burny's body. Burny fell back and turned to Pete, who, visibly astonished, tried to catch him. Burny looked up at Pete and whispered, "Why?" Milburn Palmer then slumped back on the ground and died.

The boy who shot the arrow immediately dropped his bow and said, "¡Lo siento!" Then, "I'm sorry! I didn't mean to! Slipped!"

Chris looked at the boy with scorn then turned back and pointed his finger at Joe, "That's on you," he screamed. "You done that! You done all this!" He waved his arms around him.

Joe looked at Milburn Palmer lying dead on the ground, then at Pete, then at Bradford, and finally at Diego. He placed his head all the way back and yelled as loud as he had ever yelled in his life, "Hee-yah, cattle! Git 'em up and movin'! Hee-yah, cattle" Joe then aimed his rifle at Chris Lomax and blew the top of Lomax's head off. Bits of skull and hair, and a heavy mist of blood, flew from

Lomax's head, scattering and landing on the ground behind him, followed by Lomax's lifeless body.

For an instant, everything was still. Then arrows and bullets hit Joe's body before he could cock the hammer of his carbine to get off a second shot. When Joe fell, his ear on the ground heard and felt the unmistakable sound of the hooves of two thousand cattle stampeding. Before Joseph Edwards passed away, he smiled.

Pete held up his rifle and aimed it at the nervous young Mexican who had picked up his bow and was pointing a new arrow at Pete. Pete had never shot a man before. "¡Por favor," he pleaded with the young man, "bajalo, bajalo!"

The young Mexican swallowed hard. Then he let the arrow fly. It hit Pete in the right shoulder and Pete fired twice, the second bullet striking the boy in the chest, killing him. Pete pulled the arrow out of his shoulder, winced, and turned to the men who were standing behind the man named Lomax. Shaking, he aimed his rifle at one man and fired, missing him. He cocked the hammer and tried to steady himself but before he could pull the trigger, he was shot in the back by two men firing Colt Peacemakers. Pedro Gomez fell forward and died.

Diego ran to the wagon and grabbed the shotgun he kept under the seat. He aimed at the two men who just shot his closest friend and fired both barrels. One man received the two slugs and was knocked off his feet, the other stepped back and, taking careful aim, shot Diego Martinez in the head, killing him instantly.

Among the confusion, Bradford Beaverson turned and ran to where the horses were tethered. He kicked out one of the stakes with his boot and jumped on a horse; it turned out to be Pete Gomez's favorite, a chestnut brown stallion, and Bradford rode it, bareback, into the darkness.

The man named Curtis, who had been standing next to Lomax when he was killed, looked around him. He felt that he was in charge now and began to give orders. "You," he yelled to the man who just killed Diego Martinez, "Get as many men as you can find that can ride and go after them cows." He looked at the man with the bleeding eye and the man whose nose had been broken by George Walsh and said, "Help me turn this wagon over. We're gonna torch it like proper Injuns. Hey, you over there. Kid," he said to a young man carrying a bow, "put arrows in every dead body you find."

Of the twenty-two men who were sent by Nathan Burdette to follow and rustle Stumpy Callahan's herd, nine were dead, one had a cracked skull, one had lost an eye, one had a broken jaw, and one had an arrow in his shoulder. That left nine able-bodied men to bring whatever part of the herd that could be recovered to Mexico.

Of the eleven cowhands entrusted by Stumpy Callahan to bring his herd to market in Las Animas, Colorado, all were dead except one: Bradford Beaverson.

Chapter 19

Dude's head had just stopped hurting and he was beginning to doze when Chance walked into the jailhouse and told him he had just sent a wire to Charlie Smith's wife in Laredo. "We may be getting busy the next couple of days. I don't know what's really going on with organizing any lynching party for Burke. Why don't you go get some sleep and come back for rounds later?"

Dude took his feet off Chance's desk and said okay. He stood and left the jailhouse. Chance thought to himself that he should have also told Dude to stay away from that woman.

#

To get to Carlos' hotel, Dude had to walk past the Burdette saloon. Maggie was sitting at one of the small café tables on the saloon's porch. She called to Dude and he walked up the two steps of the porch. "You didn't come to the party last night. Or afterward," she said, sipping a cup of tea.

"Yeah, well," replied Dude, "I had to go back to the jailhouse. Turns out we got a new old prisoner."

Maggie looked Dude up and down and said, "You look exhausted. Come upstairs for a rest."

Dude hesitated. He wondered who had been upstairs with her last night. But he also felt that familiar stirring for her as well. He scratched his chin.

Maggie saw the hesitation, stood, walked over to Dude and got as close as she could to him. She whispered in his ear, "Come on, darling, we need this. We need each other." She touched his chin and gently guided his face towards hers and kissed him passionately. Dude looked into her eyes. She took his hand in hers and they went up to her room.

#

When they had finished making love, Dude looked at Maggie, and said, "Why don't you stop this?"

Maggie rose and put on a silk pink robe. She picked up a hairbrush, looked in a mirror and started to comb out her hair. "Stop what, darling?" she asked.

Dude waved his arms around the room and said, "This. All this. I want you to make love because of love, not because of money. Make love with me. Only me. You make me happy and I think I make you happy. Stop all this." He waved his arms around the room again.

"I don't make love to anyone else," she responded, still combing her hair. "I do things with men for business. I've told you that. It's not always money. Not always simply money. Business is power, too. I do favors to get bigger favors. Favors that can change my circumstances – and yours, possibly – for the better. Are you so simple you can't understand that?" She put down the brush and stared at Dude.

Dude became angry. "Yeah, well I guess I'm just a simple deputy and I can only understand simple things. Things like happiness. Things like love." He rose and began to put on his pants.

Maggie was angry as well. "Yes, and things like violence," she said.

Dude was buttoning his shirt. "That's right, violence. Without it, how do you think men like Trenton and Burdette survive? The difference is that they make other people do their violence while they stay clean and white. Men like Burdette's lawyer! Yeah, I saw you with him last night. Was he in this bed?"

Maggie rose and said, "What if he was? It shouldn't make any difference to you. You had your fun right now. What more do you want?"

Dude walked over to Maggie and grabbed both her wrists, "I want you!" he yelled. "I've never loved a woman before but I know this is right and it's what I want. I want to be normal like everybody else. I want you, Maggie!" He tried to kiss her but she released his grasp and stepped back.

"Get out," she said. Dude looked pleadingly at her but she turned her back. He picked up his boots and gun belt and left the room.

Dude pulled his boots on at the top of the stairs and strapped on his guns as he descended the staircase. He tied the holsters to each leg and walked to the Long Branch. There was a large crowd at the bar surrounding a man who seemed to be holding court and making a speech. The man wore a long coat and had a gray beard. Dude went up to Dave the bartender and said, "Hey, what's going on here?"

Dave shook his head and replied, "Oh, this guy's been speechifyin' for over an hour now. Talkin' 'bout protectin' the public. Also talkin' 'bout a lynchin'. That man you got in the jail. Burke? You an' Chance may wanna be careful."

Dude glanced at the man and the crowd again then looked back at Dave. He rubbed his mouth and said, "I'm headin' up to see Stumpy again. Can you give me one of those bottles?" He laid two silver dollars on the bar.

Dave shrugged his shoulders and said, "Sure. Say hello to Stumpy for me." Dude took the bottle Dave handed him and turned to leave. The man doing all the talking noticed him.

"Why there is one of the very men it is our privilege and duty to defend," he said pointing at Dude. "A type of man that puts himself in harm's way to protect us each and every day. Friend," he said to Dude, "allow me the honor of buying you a drink and explain how I – and this austere group assembled – plan to rid you of that deadly cancer that threatens you. That malignant growth sitting in your jail under your very nose as we speak."

Dude was too angry to even focus on what the man was saying. He backed away towards the saloon doors and waved the man off. He heard the man say, "Why of course a lawman totally dedicated to protect our citizenry has little time for such triviality. God's speed to you, sir, and thank you most wholeheartedly for your service to our community. Now, gentlemen, as I was saying…"

If Dude was not so upset and was in his normal frame of mind, he would have sprinted to the jailhouse to warn Chance about all the lynching talk and mob organization. But none of that was important now. His chance of being normal, of having the things that everyone wants and should want, was quickly disappearing. He walked to Gibbs' stables and broke the seal of the bottle. He went behind the rear wall and drank directly from the bottle. That feeling, he thought, I have to destroy that feeling. I'm no good. I'm unlovable. I'm violent. I'm broken.

He put his back to the wall and slowly slid down it until he was sitting on the ground. He crossed his legs Indian-style and continued to drink from the bottle.

He looked down at the bottle still in his hand. He had drunk more than half of it and that was more that he had drunk the last time. Unlike last time, though, his head did not hurt and he did not feel tired. He felt good. He felt powerful. He stood and walked quickly to the jailhouse.

#

Dude rushed into the jailhouse. "Chance," he blurted, "They're in the bar talkin' about lynching Burke."

Chance looked up and said, "Dude, you're drunk!"

"I ain't drunk," responded Dude, "in fact, I feel great. But I'm warning you we gotta do something, and now. They'll be comin' to string him up and I'm here to help ya," and pointed at Burke's cell.

Chance stared at Dude. "You're in no shape to even help yourself."

Dude was confused: here he was coming to warn Chance and stand by his side and Chance was rejecting him. Just like Maggie rejected him. "What?" Dude managed to say to Chance.

Chance stood up and walked directly to Dude. "It's that woman," he said, "look at what she's doing to you."

Dude got angry. "She ain't a part of this. Why are you even bringing her into it? What's the problem, John T.? Maybe you're jealous of her. Maybe that's why I've never seen you with a woman —"

Chance struck him across the face with the back of his hand. "Get out, Dude. Don't come back until you sober up. Or don't come back at all."

Dude stared back at Chance. His face stung and his jaw hurt. He was at once ashamed and angry. He turned and walked out the door. He passed a crowd of men talking loudly in the street. The man with the long coat and gray beard yelled to him, "Deputy, you're one of the very men we wish to speak with..." Dude walked right past the crowd and headed towards his hotel. He was still carrying the bottle.

Chapter 20

The man named Curtis had organized the remaining men in his gang into two separate groups. Eight men were assigned to take the remaining cattle to Mexico to be sold. Due to the fury with which the cattle stampeded and the ineptitude of the amateur cowhands, less than half of the herd was recovered. The other group was to serve as surrogate Comanches, making the scene at the campsite look as if a raiding party had attacked the cowhands and murdered them. The wagon that was the responsibility of Diego Morales was overturned and set on fire. All the cowhands were stripped of their belongings, Curtis allowing his men to keep whatever they found, the rest was thrown into the flames coming from the wagon. Things like money, weapons, ammunition, tobacco, and boots were kept while almost everything else was burned. In Milburn Palmer's saddlebag, one of the men found a small book of poetry, "Leaves of Grass" written and published by someone named Walt Whitman. The book, along with some sketches, pencils and spices, were all thrown into the fire. In what he considered a clever afterthought, Curtis had Joe Edwards's body tied to one of the scorched wagon wheels, as if the trail boss had been tortured before being killed.

Curtis had counted the dead bodies of the cowhands and knew that one had escaped. It was the teen-aged Bradford Beaverson. If that boy got back to Rio Bravo with the real story of the massacre, it would mean trouble. The second major task for the surrogate Comanche group was to track down and kill the boy.

#

Bradford had ridden south since leaving the camp the night before. It was almost mid-morning and he knew he had to rest Pete Gomez's horse soon. He needed to find water and tried hard to remember the nearest stream that Ted Davis had found for the herd the day before. They had stopped at that stream less than twenty-four hours ago. And Bradford realized that all those men he was riding with then were now dead. Was this real? he thought. Did Joe Edwards and Milburn Palmer both try to save him last night? He was a coward. In the presence of truly brave men, he was a coward. He ran and they stayed and fought. And died. Then he thought about his brother, Taylor, and the fear he felt was replaced by a paralyzing sadness. Was this all real? He kept saying to himself.

To rest the back of Pedro Gomez's horse, he dismounted and led it by the reins for a while. Not only was he thirsty, he was hungry as well. Because he went right to sleep last night, he missed supper. What he wouldn't do for some of Diego Morales' scrambled eggs right now. Or a chicken leg with Milburn Palmer's barbecue sauce caked on it. Then he thought of the horse. Harper Turner was always telling him to take care of the horse first, especially when it came to water.

Because he had fallen asleep in the saddle at some points the day before, his memory of this part of the trail was sketchy. He took out his father's pocket watch, but not to tell the time. George Walsh had shown him a trick about using a watch as a compass. By holding the watch horizontally and pointing the hour hand in the direction of the sun, the angle between the hour hand and twelve o'clock mark is the north-south line. Using the watch as a guide, Bradford continued to head south-west.

He had passed the area that Ted Davis had used for the noon break the day before. It was becoming late afternoon and Bradford was beginning to despair. He felt sorry for Pedro Gomez's stallion and urged the horse on. Finally, at half-past five, he came upon the area that the cowhands used for the evening camp two nights prior. It had a wide stream running west. Bradford imagined that it spilled into the Rio Grande. He ran to the stream and dipped his bandana into the cold water then ran back to the horse and thoroughly wiped its mouth. Harper Turner would have been proud of him, he thought. He then led the horse to the stream and the two drank to their content. He sat back and remembered the night that Otis Walker had made fishing poles from some oak branches, got some twine from

Diego Morales's wagon and the two of them and his brother, Taylor, went fishing. They caught nothing that night but it was fun, especially for Taylor. He looked around for something he could use as a pole and fishing line. Because the group had tried to keep to open ground, there was little in the way of trees. He took out his pocketknife and started to cut small holes in his bandana. He then took off his belt and tied the ends of the bandana to the belt. He took off his boots, rolled up his pant legs and waded into the stream up to his calves. He opened his legs wide and then waited for a school of pike to swim by. After about ten minutes, he saw a group of dark images swimming towards him. He lowered his "net" into the water. His first attempt came up empty but his second try yielded him a small pike, slightly larger than his own hand. The fish jumped out of the bandana but Bradford was able to catch and hold on to it. He was ecstatic and ran to the shore. George Walsh had told him that the Kiowas ate raw fish but the thought made Bradford gag. He wrapped the fish in his bandana to keep the dirt and sand off it, then started a fire with two rocks and dry pine needles and sticks that he found on the edge of the stream. Once the fire started, Brad gutted and cleaned the fish and stuck his knife through it. He then cooked the fish on the open flame, turning it several times. Once he felt it was cooked to his liking, he let it cool, and ate the fish, then lay back on the ground and closed his eyes. When he awoke, it was still daylight. His father's watch told him it was almost seven o'clock. He decided to push on until nightfall. He got on Pedro Gomez's horse and continued southwest.

By his estimation, Rio Bravo was still more than four hundred miles southwest.

Chapter 21

The light knocking on the door of his room awoke Dude but he chose to ignore it. It wasn't until he heard Maggie's voice calling him did he force himself to get out of bed. His head hurt again. He walked to the door and opened it. Maggie was standing there, dressed in a long black skirt and the denim blouse she wore on their first date. It looked as if she had gotten dressed in a hurry. She was crying and her left temple was bruised. She embraced Dude and said, "I'm sorry. I'm sorry. I love you, too. Let's get away from here."

Dude held her and said. "Sure, of course." He looked at her face and became angry. "Did he hit you?"

"Yes. You were right: it's all evil and ugly and I want out of it. All of it."

Dude, who had fallen asleep fully dressed, undid his gun belt, threw it on the bed and headed for the door. Maggie grabbed his arm and said to him, "No, Dude. Let's just go. Let's just get away, far away."

Dude did not reply. He went through the door, leaving it open, and ran down the stairs. He went out the back door of the hotel and ran to Burdette's saloon.

Rudolph Trenton was standing at the bar conversing with the President of the Rio Bravo City Bank. When he saw Dude rush into the bar, he said to himself that women like Maggie deserved such treatment, perhaps even expected such treatment. Even low-level lawmen like Dude should understand that and if he didn't, he would have to explain it to him. I am not afraid of him.

When he saw the look on Dude's face as he approached, he had a complete change of mind. He turned and headed for the stairs. He had reached the third step when Dude grabbed him by the back collar of his coat and threw him backwards to the floor. When

Trenton stood up, Dude punched him in the jaw with his right fist, followed instantly by a left fist into Trenton's right cheek. Trenton fell heavily to the floor and was slow to get up. One of the faro dealers left his table and grabbed Dude by his left arm just as the bartender was grabbing Dude's right arm. Dude used the two men as support as he kicked the rising Trenton in the chest with both feet. Trenton fell backwards again and skidded across the floor. Dude, the faro dealer and the bartender all fell in one pile. Dude extracted himself from the men's grasp, stood up, pointed at Trenton lying on the floor and said, between breaths, "Don't you. Ever. Again." And walked briskly out of the bar.

The ache in Dude's head had been replaced by the throbbing in the knuckles of each of his hands. His mind was racing. He saw the mob heading towards the jailhouse and sprinted back to the hotel. He saw Carlos behind the lobby desk and said to him, "Hey, Carlos, you got any old clothes I can use? I got some dirty work to do."

"Si, Señor Dude. I bring them up to your room," replied Carlos.

Dude thanked him and ran up to the stairs, taking two at a time, and went to his room. Maggie stood and met him as he entered. "Did you do anything to him?" she asked.

"We had a conversation," answered Dude as he went to the pitcher and bowl and washed his hands and face. "That's not important now," he continued. "I got one last thing to do and then we can leave this place. Go anywhere you want. The two of us."

Maggie looked intently at Dude. "I have to go back there," she said, "I have to get my things. And my money. He owes me money."

Dude turned to her. "Why would you bend down to take money from scum like him? We don't need any of that money. I have some and I can just make more."

Maggie, with a look of deep concern, said, "How? What would you do? Still be a lawman somewhere else? I don't want to be with a lawman who can be shot in the back at any time!"

Dude stared at her, "I can do anything. Anything I want. We'll be fine." He was interrupted by Carlos knocking on the door.

#

There were more than fifty men standing outside the jailhouse and more continued to join. John T. Chance walked outside, carrying his Winchester rifle with the saddle-ring lever. "This is an illegal assembly. Disperse and go back to your homes. Now," he said to the mob.

The man in the long coat and gray beard was at the head of the crowd. "Sheriff," he began, "I am the officially appointed spokesman for the Rio Bravo Citizens Committee for the Support of Law Enforcement and I am requesting, for your own good and safety, to please stand aside and allow us to protect you. The man you are holding has shown a proven disregard and complete contempt for men of your caliber, men who have dedicated their lives to protect us citizens. I am pleading with you to allow us to return the favor and act on your behalf as advocates for justice. I reiterate, this is for your safety…"

The man's speech was interrupted by the sound of Chance's rifle being fired into the air. "No one steps foot into this jail. No one."

Some men in the crowd began to yell at Chance. One man – the man who confronted Chance just days ago on this very subject – reached to his holster and began to draw his gun. He had raised it chest high when he was hit on the back of his head with the handle of a gun held by another man. It was Dude, who had reached across two men to strike the man. Dude was dressed in a straw sombrero, musty-smelling gingham shirt and wool pants with holes and patches. When the man collapsed to the ground holding his head,

Dude spun the pistol in his hand to place it in shooting position and then drew his other pistol. He cocked them both, stepped to the outside of the crowd and pointed the guns. He kicked the man's pistol away.

"There's too many of us, Deputy," said a man in the crowd. "Even for you and Chance."

The man in the long coat and gray beard turned to Dude. "It was never our intention for this to turn violent," he began.

Another shot rang out from the other side of the crowd. Everyone turned to see a large man with a white bandage wrapped around his middle. The man was so large that the smoking gun looked as small as a derringer in his hand. In his left hand, he carried a Sharps fifty-caliber rifle. "Holy cow," said one man in the crowd, "who armed the mountain?"

Charlie Smith addressed the crowd: "I am the U.S. Marshall for this territory. That is my prisoner in there and anyone who interferes will be facing the full power of the U.S. government. If you get in my way, the second thing I will do is arrest you and charge you with a felony." He paused.

Finally, a man shouted, "What's the first thing you'd do?"

Charlie began to walk through the parting crowd, "Shoot you," he said in reply.

Chance smiled and lowered his rifle. Charlie, followed by Dude who was still pointing his guns at the crowd, walked up the steps to the jailhouse and went inside. Chance surveyed the crowd, saw that it was dispersing, then followed the other lawmen into the jailhouse. He closed the door behind him.

Chance thanked Charlie and Dude then turned to Dude and said, "But this doesn't change anything, Dude. You were just doing your job and need to keep doing it. And doing it sober."

Dude looked at Chance and said, "You're right John T., this doesn't change nothin'. I'm done. I'm leavin'. And as soon as I can." He turned to Charlie and said, "Charlie, how you gonna get Burke to Laredo? You need help?"

Charlie looked at both Dude and Chance and said, "I already wired for an escort and the office is sending three men tomorrow. Between the four of us, we should be okay. But thanks anyway, Dude."

Dude said, "Fine, Charlie," then turned to Chance and said, "I'll drop off my badge tomorrow." Dude walked out of the jailhouse.

Charlie looked at Chance and said, "What happened between you two?"

Chance replied, "Nothing that can be taken back and nothing an apology can fix."

Chapter 22

Curtis rode with the other five men in his group. Only one other man, Barney Swint from Douglasville, did not have a current injury. The man who had lost his right eye from the rock thrown by Ted Davis had a makeshift patch over it, made from a piece of leather cut from Burtrum Hayes' saddlebag. The man with the broken jaw, courtesy of yet another rock thrown by Ted Davis, had a yellow bandana supporting his chin, knotted at the top of his head. The man Ted Davis had shot in the shoulder with an arrow had an improvised sling that was once Diego Morales's plaid linen shirt. The man whose skull was fractured and nose broken by George Walsh still had the pant leg from the longjohn underwear wrapped around his head. The "bandage" was no longer white but brown with dirt and dust.

This is some bunch I'm leading, thought Curtis to himself. But as pitiful as they were, that boy from Rio Bravo should prove no match for them. We will find that kid, kill him, then head back to Burdette's ranch to settle up. He was planning on telling Burdette that the remaining men should also get shares of the pay set aside for the dead men as reward for surviving this whole mess. Chris had been right about that, at least. Joe Edwards should have given up the herd the second those arrows started. Stubborn son-of-a-bitch. But so what if it meant more money in my pocket, he thought.

Barney turned to Curtis, "Are you sure we headed right?" he asked.

Curtis was annoyed with the question. "We headed south, ain't we? That boy is running back to his mama and he headed south, too."

#

Bradford Beaverson was letting Pete Gomez's horse graze in the same field the herd had passed through three days ago. Bradford had been able to catch rabbits by setting up an intricate spring trap using his pocketknife, his belt and one of his boots. His boots had turned out to be very handy. Since he did not have a canteen, he used his boots to carry water for him and the horse. He tied the two of them together using the pulls and slung them over the horse's neck. If he could go on catching rabbits and squirrels, as well as consistently finding water and using his "net" to catch fish, he felt he could make it back to Rio Bravo in another two weeks. His confidence seemed to be getting stronger by the hour. His biggest regret now was that he had not been able to grab a blanket when he ran from the camp. At night, he would awake several times, shivering violently and uncontrollably. Once, he lay on the horse's back for warmth but fell to the ground after rolling over in a deep sleep.

#

Curtis and his group, on the other hand, were running low on provisions. Since Chris ordered the wagon burned, the group – as well as the other set of men sent to Mexico with the remainder of the herd – could only bring what they could carry. In their haste to pursue Bradford Beaverson, the band overlooked the ample provisions Diego Morales still had on hand. Much of the salted beef, vegetables, canned fruit, and coffee were left behind. When the wagon was overturned, the crate containing the live chickens was smashed and the birds were released. The men were so preoccupied in destroying the campsite that they did not even think to try to catch them.

"Hey," said the man who was missing an eye, "I'm hungry. Who has jerky?"

"I got jerky," said the man with the arrow tip still in his shoulder. "But my canteen's almost empty. Wanna trade?"

"Sure," said the first man, "We'll be coming on water soon but I doubt we'll be coming up on any jerky."

#

Employing the tracking tip George Walsh had once told him, Bradford was following cattle droppings to backtrack his way home. Bradford knew exactly where he was: it was the spot that the exhausted cattle had stopped after the stampede. His brother, Taylor Beaverson, along with Harper Turner and Otis Walker, were buried along the nearby stream. He dismounted his horse. He had become used to riding bareback, getting off and walking more often than on a saddle. It was good rest for both him and the horse. "T.S.," he said to the horse, "over there is where my brother lies." He decided to call Pete Gomez's horse "Taylor the Second," in honor of his brother. Saying "Taylor," though, made him sad so he started to just call him, "T.S." He led T.S. to the graves. There were no markers. They had been buried in the order that their bodies were found. Taylor Beaverson was the first one on the right, Harper Turner in the middle, and Otis Walker on the left. Bradford squatted by the grave on the right. "Hey, little brother," he said, "You sure did miss a hell of a commotion. It was bloody and ugly and scary. I been thinkin' on it a lot and think maybe you was the lucky one what didn't have to see it." He stood and picked up a flat stone nearby and skimmed it across the stream. "Hey, Tayl," he exclaimed, "six skips! How 'bout that? Betcha could never beat that." Then he paused as he realized just how true that statement was. He wiped tears from his eyes. "I'll tell Ma how brave you was. And what a good hand you became. Good-bye, Taylor." Bradford turned and got his boots from around T.S.'s neck and filled them in the stream. He had a thought that the water may taste sweeter now that his brother was so nearby.

Heading south, Bradford was familiar with the next area, as well. It was the area that Taylor Beaverson had been trampled by a stampeding herd. He saw the several dead steer in the distance, arrows sticking out of them, their carcasses rotting in the sun. He had a fleeting thought to cut some meat for him and T.S. but knew that it was all spoiled by now. He thought about skinning one of the cows for blankets for T.S. and himself. The nights had been cold and a warm hide would help. But the flies buzzing around the hides told him that the bodies were maggot-ridden by now. He saw vultures gnawing and tearing away at one steer in the far distance. Although the sun was beginning to set, Bradford wanted to get past this area before setting up camp for the night. If he followed the original trail established by Ted Davis he would once again be near "cover," as Joe Edwards put it, meaning apple and pear trees, and berry bushes. It would also mean ample wood for fires. This would be the easier part of the journey, Bradford said to himself.

#

Unbeknownst to Curtis and his group, they were not actually following Bradford Beaverson. The group was heading due south while Bradford's course was southwest, on a clear path to Rio Bravo. In another one hundred miles, the group would be at the outskirts of Fort Concho. The trip north was easier because they simply tracked the herd and did not bother to collectively identify landmarks.

Barney Swint rode up to Curtis, who was leading the group. "Curtis," he said in a low tone, "I don't recognize anything around here. We shoulda caught up to that kid by now."

"Yeah, well," responded Curtis, "For all we know, he could be dead by now. He left with nothin' near as I could tell. He starved or died of thirst I reckon. If he is alive and if we don't come up on 'im, we got to at least beat him back to Bravo. Let's get to the nearest town and get our bearings."

#

It was morning and Bradford had just woken up, shivering. He had found cover the night before in a patch of forest that had raspberry bushes nearby. He built another fire while breakfasting on a handful of berries. He looked up and saw a cloud of dust in the distance. He then heard the rumble of hoof beats. That couldn't be our herd, he thought to himself; ours had to be three times as large. He could barely make out the silhouettes of cowboys tending the herd. If those were our cattle – Stumpy's cattle – or what's left of them, he thought to himself, what would Joe Edwards want him to do? Take them back? Follow the herd to find the rustlers' destination? Get help from the law to pursue the herd? Certainly the first option was out of the question. Singlehandedly and without any weapons, overcoming those cowboys and taking back the herd was surely an impossible feat. If he followed them, what could he do once they stopped? His only choice was to get help, preferably from the authorities. But he still didn't know for a fact if they were Stumpy's cattle. The only way to know for sure was to get close enough to see the brand. He decided to mount T.S. and follow the herd.

#

Bradford had been tracking the herd for about five miles. He was able to determine that, even from a distance, the cows were Herefords, just like Stumpy's. He thought the skills of the tending cowboys were lacking and wished Burtrum Hayes or Pete Gomez or Milburn Palmer was there to see all the mistakes these hands were making. They didn't even bother to go after strays. That is when Bradford got the idea to go after one of the strays himself to verify whether or not the Herefords had Stumpy's brand.

He did not have to wait long as he saw one steer amble off to the left of the herd towards a ravine. Bradford led T.S. to the left and followed. It took him almost an hour to find it. He dismounted and approached the cow, humming quietly to it. He saw the brand on its right hindquarter: a large capital C (for Callahan), with a joined P and M (Patrick and Malachy) written in script, connected to the middle of the C. Bradford stroked the brand and turned to leave. A cowboy on horseback was staring at him, his left hand resting on his pistol handle. Just my luck, thought Bradford: the one stray they decide to go after was the one I followed.

Thinking quickly back to the few Spanish lessons Diego Martinez had conducted on the drive for both he and Taylor,

Bradford looked askingly to the cowboy, "Por favor. Aqua. Aqua," and pointed to his mouth.

The cowboy looked down at Bradford's bare feet. He hesitated a moment. "Poor wretch," he finally said, "Here," and threw one of the canteens that was flung over his saddle horn to Bradford. "Now, git."

Bradford immediately recognized the canteen as Milburn Palmer's. More than once on the drive, he had offered it to Bradford. Continuing with the charade, Bradford opened the canteen and drank as if he was dying of thirst. He then muttered, "Gracias, gracias, señor," and walked quickly to T.S., mounted and galloped off.

#

The man with the arrowhead in his shoulder spotted a building to the south and called to Curtis, "Hey, I think I found a town!" He pointed in the distance. Curtis used George Walsh's telescope to view the building. He nodded and the group galloped towards the two-story frame house. Once they reached the building, they discovered that it was the only one in the area, sandwiched between two water tanks. Behind the house were a set of sand hills and an unfinished railroad track lay about one hundred yards in front of it.

The men dismounted and tied up their horses. They entered the building to find two long wooden tables and a makeshift bar comprised of boards nailed into a pair of stacked crates on either end. A very pretty, middle-aged woman in a long calico dress covered by a gingham apron came out of a room that must have served as the kitchen. "Why, lookatcha'all," she said pleasantly.

Curtis touched his hat brim with his left hand and said, "Howdy, Missus. Can I ask – just where we are? I mean, what is the name of this town?"

The woman smiled, "Oh, I don't think we're a town just yet but I guess you can call it Monahans after the man who founded it."

Curtis replied, "Well, would you be Missus Monahans then?"

The woman shook her head, "Oh, no. My name is Mollie Dawson and my family and a few others live here. Most of the men work for the railroad. But I guess you can consider this a combination hotel, bar and restaurant, depending on what y'all need."

Curtis looked at the other men. "Well, beer would be good, if you got some. Whiskey'd be better. And we'll all pretty hungry. Ya got eggs, steak, beans?"

Molly pointed to one of the long tables and said, "Sure, we got all those things. Sit down and we'll set y'all up." She went behind the bar and pulled out a bottle of whiskey, grabbed a handful of glasses and put them all down in the middle of the first table. The man with the broken jaw watched her greedily. She ignored his glance to ask, "Would you be needin' rooms, then?"

Curtis, who had taken the role of spokesman for the group, responded, "No, Missus, just passing through."

Molly went into the kitchen and yelled, "Steaks, eggs, beans for six men. Caitlin, get some beer out there, too. Hurry, then!"

A young girl, no older than fourteen, with yellow hair and deep-set blue-green eyes, came out with a pitcher of beer in each hand. She set them on the first table. The man with the broken jaw nudged the man with the cracked skull and pointed with his swollen chin in the direction of the girl.

Molly stood in the doorway of the kitchen, observing the men. "So, then," she said, "where are y'all headed?"

At first, Curtis looked at the floor, embarrassed. Then he looked up at Molly with a degree of confidence and said, "Rio Bravo way."

Molly had a perplexed look on her face. "Rio Bravo?" she said, "Why that's the Rio Grande! It's gotta be two hundred miles west. Southwest, in fact. Where are ya comin' from?"

Curtis first looked at the face of each of the men before responding. "Colorado. We brought a herd to market up there. A couple of us got hurt in the journey. Accidents mostly. Damn cows. Too stupid and unpredictable." He then stood up. "We may have gone off course. Would you have a map we could look at?"

Molly did not move right away. "Perhaps himself has one. I'll go check." She turned to the kitchen. "Hurry with that food now."

A young boy, perhaps a year younger than the girl, came out of the kitchen carrying two plates, each containing a large steak, two sunny-side-up eggs, and a small mound of baked beans. He placed one in front of Curtis and the other in front of Barney Swint. The man who was missing an eye grabbed the boy by the arm and demanded, "Where's mine?"

The boy looked down and replied, "It—it—it's c-c-c-c-coming, s-s-s-sir," and ran back to the kitchen. He came back out almost immediately with two more identical plates and laid one in front of the man with the missing eye.

The man laughed at the boy and said, mockingly, "Th-th-th-at's b-b-better!" He then grabbed the steak with both hands and began to tear at it with his teeth.

Molly had been observing this from the bottom of the staircase. She was holding a map in her hands and cradled a long-barreled shotgun in the nook of her left arm. "Right," she said, "here is a map of the territory for your use. You can't take it with yas, though." Her manner and tone had changed from friendly to business-like. "The master of the house will be down momentarily."

Curtis put down his knife and fork, went over to Molly and took the map. He called Barney over and the two of them studied it. Barney offered to trace it and asked Molly for a pencil and paper. Molly went to the desk on the side of the bar, placed the shotgun on top of it, reached into one of the drawers and produced a grease pencil and a piece of brown wrapping paper. "You can use these, I guess," she said.

Curtis smiled at Molly and walked towards the bar. By then, the young boy appeared with the last two plates. Curtis said to Molly, "Is that the master's shotgun or yours?"

Molly straightened up and replied, "Right: six suppers, beer, one bottle of whiskey. That'll be twenty-five dollars." She put her hand on the shotgun.

Curtis gave out a small laugh. "Well, let us finish then we can settle up. How's that?" Without waiting for a reply, he sat back down at his plate and poured a shot of whiskey. He drank the whiskey in one gulp then drank an entire glass of beer immediately after. He cut into his steak and looked over at the man with the arrowhead in his shoulder sitting directly across from him and winked.

In a single motion, Curtis grabbed the side of his plate with his right hand and flung it at Molly's head, the steak flew off across the room. Molly, anticipating such a move, grabbed the shotgun and ducked underneath the plank that served as the bar. The man with the arrowhead in his shoulder stood up, drew his pistol and aimed at Molly. Molly cocked the hammer of one of the shotgun barrels and shot the man in the chest. He fell backwards into the second long table. Molly then knelt on one knee and, using the top of the bar for support, fired the second barrel at Curtis, who immediately dove under the second long table behind him. Molly stood up, ran towards the door and went to the outside of the doorway. She reached into the front of her corset, took out two shotgun shells and reloaded.

The man with the broken jaw ran into the kitchen. Seeing the young girl hiding behind a large wooden tub filled with dirty dishes, he grabbed her from behind and fell down on top of her. He began to pull up her dress and undo his pants. The young boy appeared out of the side entrance of the kitchen with a twelve-inch meat cleaver. With all of his strength, the boy brought the cleaver down between the man's neck and right collarbone, just above the shoulder blade. The man's head tilted to the left and then forward. The boy stepped to the side and brought the cleaver down again on the back of the man's neck, severing the man's head halfway. The man collapsed on top of the screaming girl. The boy kicked the man's body over and helped the sobbing girl up, her dress almost completely covered with the man's blood. He was escorting her to the back staircase leading to the second floor when the man with the bandaged head walked into the kitchen. Seeing the body on the floor, the man looked up at the boy and charged him. Shooing the girl up the stairs, the boy turned and jammed the cleaver into the middle of the man's chest. The boy then took a hot frying pan off the stove and, using both hands, struck the man with the inside of it exactly in the middle of the man's bandage. With hot grease pouring off his head and blood dripping from his chest, the man fell to his knees. The boy ran out the side exit of the kitchen and to the front of the building. He went to the large triangular dinner bell hanging in the front and began ringing it. A man tarring a section of the water tower on the right stopped what he was doing, grabbed his rifle and descended the ladder leading to the ground, he then ran to the front of the building. Another man, wearing a leather apron and forging a piece of iron on the other side of the railroad tracks, put down his hammer, grabbed his rifle and went sprinting to the front of the building as well.

Molly waited by the side of the doorway and the man with the one eye came walking out, his pistol drawn. Molly waited until the man was in front of her, cocked one barrel of the shotgun and shot the man in the back. He fell, face first, into the dirt.

The man who was tarring the water tower arrived first. "What's happening, Molly? Are you all right? Are you hurt?"

Molly cocked the second barrel, looked at the man and said, "Scum. I never should have served them. It's my fault. I just should have told them to move on."

The second man arrived and, in a very heavy Irish accent, said to Molly, "What about Caitlin and Kieran? Are they okay? Was it Kieran who rang the bell?" The other man indicated with his rifle Kieran standing by the dinner bell. The second man shot a glance inside the building then ran to the boy.

"Are ya hurt, son?" Asked the man and put his arm around the boy. Kieran shook his head. "Okay. Good. Where's your sister?" Kieran pointed to the second story and the man said, "Let's get you upstairs with her then." The man held Kieran back while he peered into the kitchen from the side entrance. When the man saw the two dead bodies, he looked quizzically at Kieran, then hugged him and kissed him on top of his head. "Sure," the man whispered, "you've done a man's work today, lad. Now go upstairs and don't come down till we call ya." The boy ran up the back staircase and the man went back to the front of the building.

"Looks like Kieran got two of 'em," the man said.

"Jesus, Mary and Joseph," exclaimed Molly, making the sign of the cross. "That means there's just two of 'em."

The first man turned to Molly and said, "Stay back, Moll. We'll take it from here." He told the other man to go back to the side entrance. Once the man with the leather apron had reached that point, the first man yelled into the building, "You in there, we've the place surrounded. Come out with your hands in the air and we won't have to kill yas."

Barney looked at Curtis, he was still holding the copy of the map. "What do we do, Curtis?" he whispered.

With a nod of his chin, Curtis indicated to Barney to stand and give themselves up. When Barney stood, Curtis yelled, "No, no!" then took out his pistol and fired at the open door. He then lay down on the floor, spreading his arms in front of him.

Repeatedly cocking the lever of his Winchester rifle, the first man shot Barney Stint four times.

The second man, with his rifle ready, entered the room from the kitchen. He called to the front door, "I think they're all dead. I think that last feller may have killed the utter one." Molly and the man walked into the front with their rifles cocked. They looked at the bodies on the floor. "Maybe we should start in the kitchen. Bit of a mess there."

When Molly and the two men went into the kitchen, Curtis jumped up, grabbed the copy of the map from Barney Stint's lifeless hand and shoved it in his shirt. He ran out the front of the building, got on his horse and headed west.

Chapter 23

Dude and Maggie awoke together in Dude's hotel room. Dude reached over and began to roll a cigarette. Maggie got out of bed and grabbed the bottle of whiskey. Smiling at Dude, she asked, "Too early for a drink?"

Dude returned the smile and said, "Why not? I don't have to go to work." He lit the cigarette as Maggie lay next to him carrying the bottle and one glass. "Where's my glass?" he said.

"Oh," said Maggie, "Have you grown up? You don't need the momma bird to feed you anymore?" She poured whiskey in the glass and took a sip. She then kissed Dude.

Dude kissed her a second time and said, "Well, it does add to the flavor, I have to admit. But I think I have my wings now. He kissed her again, got up and took the second glass from the dressing table. He held out the glass to Maggie and she poured him a drink then poured herself a second one.

Maggie pulled her knees to her chin and said, "I've got to get dressed and go over to Burdette's to get my things. Just one small consideration: where are we headed?"

"Anywhere," said Dude. North – Denver, Kansas City. South to Mexico. We can go back East to St. Louis…"

Maggie interrupted him. "No, not St Louis. Burned bridges. And just what do you plan to do? I already told you I don't want you to be a lawman. And how much call is there for an honest faro dealer?"

Dude looked at his empty glass. "Being asked to be a dishonest one is why I left Buford. I can play the other side of the table and do well. I think. Anyway, let's not worry about that right now. I gotta get dressed myself and hand Chance my badge." He poured another drink. "Do you want me to go over to Burdette's with you?" He put on his shirt and pants.

"Better not," she replied. "Knowing Rudy, he doesn't like to be embarrassed in public. Bad for business. I wouldn't be surprised if he has men waiting for you. And since you don't have a badge to hide behind anymore…"

Dude looked at Maggie and said, "Is that what you think? They respected the badge and not the man behind it?" He began to pull on his boots

Maggie began to get dressed. "No, darling," she said. "I just mean you don't have the power of the law behind you anymore. That's all." She went over and kissed him. "Let's go out together," she said.

When the two were dressed, Maggie and Dude left the hotel and, hand in hand, walked down the main street. They came upon Burdette's saloon and Burdette and Trenton were standing in the doorway. Trenton's left cheek was swollen and bruised. He and Dude stared at each other. Maggie kissed Dude and said, "I'll see you in a little while." She entered the saloon and walked up the flight of stairs.

Giving Trenton once last look, Dude continued towards the jailhouse. Trenton and Burdette walked into the street and watched him. Once Dude reached the jailhouse, the two men walked back into the saloon.

Chance was sitting at his desk when Dude entered. Dude held out his badge and said, "Here, John T., just as I promised. And I want to say that I'm sorry…"

Chance interrupted him, "Dude, Trenton and Burdette were just here. Trenton issued a complaint against you for assault. Assault by a law officer."

Dude began to say, "But I wasn't wearing the badge – " when Chance interrupted him.

"It doesn't matter, Dude. You were still a deputy at the time. My advice is to leave town; you were planning on that already. As far as they're concerned, I didn't see you."

Dude sat down in the chair opposite the desk. "Too late. They just saw me walk in here." He stared at the floor.

Both men were silent for a while until Dude stood up and began to take off his gun belt. "Okay, John T.," he said, "No sense you getting in trouble as well. The only choice we got is for you to lock me up. Who knows, maybe it will do me some good."

Chance stared at Dude and said, "Well, I can't hold you long for assault, even if it is for a peace officer. Maybe in a day or so it will all quiet down and I can let you out." He stood and opened the cell door. Dude handed him his folded gun belt and his hat, then walked in and sat on the cell's cot. From the other cell, Ned Burke could be heard laughing.

"'Bout time, you prancing gun-slingin' sissy," yelled Burke. "I wished he put ya in here with me!"

Charlie Smith walked in, reading a telegram. Without looking up, he said, "John, it looks like Burke's escorts will be here tomorrow – " When Charlie looked up and saw Dude in a cell, he looked at Chance and said, "I knew you two weren't getting along, but ain't this a might excessive?"

#

Maggie was putting her clothes in her blue canvas suitcase when Trenton entered her room. "So, this is how we part," he said to her.

Maggie did not look up and began to place her jewelry box in the suitcase. "Randy, you knew this couldn't go on forever. We're done. I'm moving on. Don't even think about stopping me." She turned to him. "And you owe me money."

Trenton smiled and said, "No, I don't plan on stopping you. Go and run off with your lawman. Once he's out of jail that is."

Maggie became angry. "What did you do?" she said. "Have him put in jail because he slapped you around? Because, unlike you, he hits men and not women? And if you ever touch me again, I'll have him kill you!"

Trenton laughed. "I never knew that was your type. Anyway, I have your money but there is one more gambol we have to perform. After that, we can part amicably."

Chapter 24

Riding T.S., Bradford Beaverson looked around and saw familiar sites. Every landmark – hill, stream, and tree – seemed to be welcoming him. He had just passed through the site where the herd had been stopped and camp made on the first night of the drive. He knew that in a few short hours he would be where they had all stopped for the first noon rest. From there, it was a few miles to Stumpy's ranch and just another mile and a half to home. He wondered whether he should stop at Stumpy's first and tell him what had happened, or visit his mother and explain about Taylor. The practical side of him was telling him to go directly to Stumpy so that they can get the law involved, maybe even get back that part of the herd that was stolen. His emotions told him to go to see his mother and ask forgiveness for not doing more to save Taylor. He desperately wanted to see his mother and knew she wanted to see him as well. As he passed through the part of the trail where he went after his first stray, his mind continued to weigh each of the choices.

#

As Curtis raced his horse further west, his own mind was obsessed with conjuring up just the right story to tell Nathan Burdette. Joe Edwards' cowboys had decided to make a stand and Chris Lomax had abandoned the Indian plan and had foolishly led a charge against them. When Lomax was killed by Joe Edwards, Curtis immediately took over as leader. Curtis devised and executed a successful plan that allowed his group to overpower and take the herd. In order to leave no witnesses, he was forced to kill all of Edwards' cowhands. It was unfortunate but it had to be done in order to protect Burdette. In order to keep to the plan, Curtis had made it look as if Kiowas had carried out the raid. Curtis had organized a group of Burdette men to take the herd to Mexico. Curtis also thought that he would ask Burdette for a bonus.

#

It was getting close to dusk so Bradford dismounted and led T.S. until sunset. He remembered the large pond that the cowboys had passed on the first full day of the drive and planned to make camp there. The grass by the pond was high enough for T.S. to graze, and there was a group of oak trees from which he could snap off a branch to use as a fishing pole. He had collected enough thread from his shirts to use as line and sharpened pieces of steel he had found on this trip home to use as hooks. Once he found a place for camp, he would dig for bloodworms. Milburn Palmer's canteen had come in handy since Bradford no longer had to use his boots to carry water. He had collected a bunch of mushrooms he had found that morning. Diego Morales had shown him how to tell edible from poisonous ones. Bradford has placed about a dozen in his worn and tattered bandana. He found a spot by the pond and set up his camp, gathering wood for the fire and preparing his fishing pole. His only problem remained the cold at night. No matter how much wood he put on the fire before falling asleep, the fire would die while he was asleep and he would awake completely chilled. As a result, he had developed a cough deep within his chest.

#

Curtis had been riding his own horse too hard. The horse slowed and finally came to a complete stop. "What the hell's wrong with you, nag?" said Curtis as he dismounted. He looked at each of the horse's hooves but found no cuts around the worn shoes. Reluctantly, Curtis decided to stop for the day and give both of them some rest. He took his rifle out of its scabbard and walked to a nearby grove, leading the horse by its reins. In the last two days of riding, he had only been able to shoot a single squirrel. The rifle shot had torn the animal apart so badly that Curtis could only extract small pieces and short strings of meat from its bones. He had finished the jerky in his saddlebag after the first night. He seemed to be constantly hungry. Curtis saw a small coyote in the grove, dropped the horse's rein, took aim and fired. He missed and the coyote, as well as some rabbits and squirrels, scattered further into the grove. "Damn it," yelled Curtis. He pulled the horse to a tree and tied the reins around a branch. He did not take off the horse's saddle. He lay on the ground and pulled out the copy of the map from inside his shirt. He spread it on the ground and tried to determine exactly where he was. Barney had done a good job in tracing the map: he had sketched landmarks like mountains, hills, bodies of water, and had written in the names of most towns on the way to Rio Bravo. Based on the closest landmarks, Curtis figured he was still more than one hundred miles from Burdette's ranch.

#

When the sun rose, Bradford got up from the bed of grass and pine needles that he had made the night before, took off the flannel shirt he used as a blanket and shook it. As much as he tried to warm himself at night, he awoke cold and felt unrested. His cough was getting noticeably worse, especially in the morning. He went to the tree where he had tied T.S. for the night and led him to the pond. While T.S. drank, Bradford urinated on a nearby pine bush. The fire from the night before had gone out and he started another. He took one of the black catfish he had caught the day before and put his knife through it. He placed the fish on the two slingshot-shaped sticks that he had planted on either side of the fire. While his breakfast was cooking, he knelt down next to T.S., washed his face and filled Milburn Palmer's canteen. Getting the canteen allowed him to put his boots back on. No matter how long he put them near the fire, though, the boots never seemed to come completely dry. As a result, Bradford's feet were constantly cold.

Bradford had figured that in another day and a half, he would be at Stumpy's ranch. He had decided the night before to go there first before going home to see his mother.

Chapter 25

Maggie walked into the jailhouse while Chance and Charlie Smith were planning the trip to escort Ned Burke to Laredo. "May I see Dude?" she asked Chance politely.

Chance stood up from his desk. "Sure. You can go right ahead."

"Thank you, Sheriff," said Maggie coolly. Dude stood up and held the cell bars as she walked over to his cell. "Are you okay?" she asked Dude.

"Yeah, I'm fine," replied Dude.

Maggie held one of Dude's hands and said, "I've talked to Rudy. I think I convinced him to drop the charge. I'm so sorry for this. I feel it's my fault." She took out her flask, turned to Chance and said, "May I give him this?"

Chance nodded and said, "Sure but you can't leave him with it. He can have a drink if he wants."

Maggie handed Dude the flask and he drank from it. Before handing it back, he took a second drink. Ned Burke rose from his bunk in the next cell and yelled, "Hey, what about me? Can't I get a swig?" Maggie looked at Chance.

"It's up to you," Chance said to Maggie. "But the same rule applies. He can't have the flask."

Maggie said, "I'm rather low on this." Maggie produced a pint whiskey bottle from her handbag and said, "But I guess I can afford to spare some of this." She looked at Burke and asked, "Do you have a cup?" Burke nodded, grabbed the metal cup from the side of his cot and stuck it through the bars towards Maggie. She poured from the bottle and filled the cup almost to the brim.

"Thank you, ma'am," said Burke. "You are the only one who has shown me any kindness these past weeks. God bless you." He drank quickly from the cup. "Now that's whiskey!" he exclaimed.

Maggie smiled politely at Burke than turned to Dude. "I'm going back to talk to Randy again," she said. "Do you need anything, darling?"

Dude shook his head and replied, "I just wanna get out of here and get this town behind us."

Maggie left the jailhouse as Dude sat down on his cot. Burke let out a loud belch and lay down on his own cot to finish his drink.

In a little while, Randolph Trenton and Nathan Burdette's lawyer walked into the jailhouse. "Sheriff," said the lawyer, "I have been in council with my client, Mr. Trenton here, and he wishes to drop any and all charges against Mr. Warren. Provided, however, that Mr. Warren agrees to leave the county at his earliest disposal. In order to avoid any other potential violent acts, we feel that this, coupled with a temporary restraining order, is the wisest course of action for all parties involved."

Dude jumped up when he heard this and said, "You got a deal. Chance, let me out and I'll leave this minute! I won't even pack."

Chance reached into the top drawer of his desk and produced a set of papers. "That's fine," he said. "I just need you to sign this and I can let Dude out." Trenton reached down and signed the papers while Chance grabbed the key to the cell and opened Dude's cell door. Dude walked out of the cell.

"Well," said Dude, "So long, Chance," and stuck out his hand.

Chance shook Dude's hand and said, "Take care of yourself, Dude."

Dude waved to Charlie Smith and stepped around Trenton and the lawyer.

#

Maggie was waiting outside. Dude embraced her and they kissed passionately. "Let's just go to Gibbs' and get the horses, saddle up and go. You got everything you need?"

Maggie nodded and said, "You have what you need?"

Dude grabbed her hand and said, "I do now!" They walked quickly, hand in hand, towards the stables.

#

Dude and Maggie were passed by three men on horseback heading towards the jailhouse. The three men dismounted and walked in just as Trenton and the lawyer were leaving. Charlie stood up and recognized two of the men. "Jack, Walter! Good to see you guys," he said, extending his hand.

The man named Walter said, "Hiya, Charlie. This here's Matt McGovern, sworn in just yesterday for the ride. Do ya think you can get it right and get it done this time?" The men laughed. Charlie introduced Chance to each of the men and they shook hands.

Charlie said, "I got the papers. Or I should say I still got the papers? There's the prisoner over there." The men grabbed chairs and sat around Chance's desk. Charlie opened a map and the men planned the route they would take back to Laredo. They discussed the precautions they would use in escorting Ned Burke and the roles and responsibilities of each man. When they were satisfied with the plan, Chance grabbed the cell keys again and walked up to Burke's cell.

"Okay, Burke," said Chance, "Time to get up and leave. Don't tell me you couldn't handle one drink." Chance walked into the cell and shook Burke but the man did not move. Chance rolled him over and saw vomit trickling out of Burke's mouth. "Charlie," yelled Chance, "better come in here and look at this."

Charlie Smith walked into the cell and bent down to look at Burke. "Too late for the Doc," he said looking up top Chance. "He's dead."

Chapter 26

Bradford Beaverson rode J.S. onto Stumpy's ranch at about four o'clock in the afternoon. Bradford was exhausted. He realized that he had fallen asleep several times the last few miles but even when he told himself to stay alert, he drifted back to sleep.

Stumpy was putting horses into their stables when he spotted Bradford. T.S. was slowly walking towards the corral. Stumpy walked over to the horse as fast as he could. "Is that you, Bradford Beaverson?" he called.

Bradford had fallen asleep again but awoke when he heard his name. "Stumpy?" he said weakly. He was overjoyed but even the thought of cheering exhausted him. He managed a weak laugh before allowing himself to be taken by Stumpy as he fell into his arms. Stumpy carried Bradford into his ranch house and brought him into his own bedroom. He lay Bradford down in his own bed.

"Jesus, Brad," whispered Stumpy, "you weigh next to nothin' and ya all wore out. I'll get ya some water and can ya eat anything?" Before getting an answer from Bradford, Stumpy went into the kitchen and came back with a glass of water and a loaf of bread. "Here, Brad take some of this." He laid the glass on the bedside table and broke the bread into pieces. He stood and watched as Brad slowly grabbed a piece of bread and bit into it. He took the glass of water   and   looked   up   at   Stumpy.

"The herd," said Brad, weakly, "the herd and Taylor. I'm sorry."

Stumpy quieted Brad by saying, "Not now, son. Eat more. Drink." Stumpy looked at Bradford and scratched at his beard. "Brad, I'm gonna hitch up my wagon and get the Doc. On the way, I'll drop in and fetch your Ma." Stumpy walked quickly out of the room.

#

Marjory Beaverson was sweeping her front porch when Stumpy Callahan and Doc Fix came riding up in Stumpy's wagon. "Get in, Marjory," yelled Stumpy, "It's your boy, Brad. He's back from the drive and he's at my place."

Marjory Beaverson dropped her broom, put her hands to her mouth and said, "Bradford? Thank the heavens. Was Taylor with him?"

Stumpy struggled to keep the horses in place and said, "Just him. Reckon we'll find out about Taylor soon enough. Now come on."

#

When they got back to Stumpy's ranch, Marjory Beaverson ran to the front door, ignoring the offers from Doc Fix and Stumpy to help her down off the wagon. She ran into Stumpy's bedroom and over to the bedside. Bradford was unconscious. She took Bradford's hand and put it to her cheek. Stumpy and the doctor entered the room.

"Okay, Marjory," said Stumpy, "Let's have the Doc look 'im over." He put his arms around her and escorted her out of the room. They went to the parlor and sat on the matching wing chairs.

After a while, Doc Fix came out and said to them, "It's a high fever, most likely pneumonia. He's got some bumps and bruises, nothing serious, just probably from the ride. He apparently soiled himself over the last couple of days, and his boots were pretty moldy on the inside so his feet are a bit of a mess. I cleaned him up best I could. I can't just yet figure out the stomach problems. Could be some kind of bacteria from whatever he's been livin' on these last few days. Stumpy, what'd you give him when you found him?"

Stumpy replied, "Just some well water and some bread I just took out of the stove. What I eat most of the time."

Doc shook his head in thought. "Right now I'm more concerned with the fever. He's young. That's on his side, at least. Can he stay here for now, Stump? I don't want to move him."

"Why, sure," replied Stumpy. "You're welcome too, Marjory. Want to use my wagon to get back to town, Doc?"

Doc nodded and said, "I'll bring it back later, Stumpy. I want to get some things from the office, read up on a couple of things. And I want to bring back something to bring that fever down and maybe rid him of any infection. I won't be long."

Stumpy asked Marjory Beaverson if she wanted tea. She shook her head looked down into her lap. "I'd just like to know where Taylor is," she said.

"And the others, for that matter," said Stumpy. "I think that may have been one of Pete's horses he come in on. No saddle or even a blanket, now that I think of it. Brad musta left in a hurry from wherever he was. I was gonna go into town to see if Joe wired but maybe we can get the story straight from Bradford. Maybe."

Chapter 27

Maggie and Dude were riding at a slow pace, heading west. "Well, Lawman," said Maggie, "As your prisoner I demand to know where you are taking me." She smiled at him.

Dude smiled back and said, "You're no more a prisoner than I am a lawman. But I have been thinking on it. How about across the Grande into Nuevo Laredo? The 'New' Laredo? A new town, a new country, a new start?"

Maggie nodded her head and looked at Dude, "I do believe that you have the soul of a poet, Mr. Warren."

Dude laughed and said, "I don't know about that but they speak American, it's close, there's a good hotel, and money to be made. Opportunity. But let's get settled there first. There's a chapel in the middle of the town, real pretty. We can get married – "

Maggie interrupted him, "Hold on there, Deputy. Maybe I don't want to be 'Mrs. Dude' right off. Come to think of it, what is your first name anyway?"

Dude blushed and looked down. "Howard," he said. "A very popular name from where I come from. I was named after an uncle…"

Maggie stopped her horse and laughed out loud. "'Howard?'" she yelled. "Howard Warren! Oh, your father must have hated you! You're better off with Dude. You got lucky." She continued to laugh and shook her head, "Mrs. Howard Warren? No, sir, that won't do. That won't do a'tall." She laughed even harder.

Dude was becoming angry. "Okay," he said, "you had your laugh. Are we agreed it's Nuevo Laredo?"

Maggie's laugh was slowly subsiding as she shook her head and replied, "Sure, Howard. Let's go to Mexico."

They were silent for the rest of the journey to Nuevo Laredo. After crossing over a wide wooden bridge that spanned the Rio Grande, they came upon the small but well-appointed town of Nuevo Laredo. In the middle of the town square stood a three-story cathedral, made of adobe brick and covered in white stucco. At the top of the cathedral was a gold cross, almost twelve feet high. There was a hotel to the left of the cathedral, it was named El Hotel de Oro. Maggie and Dude rode up to the hotel, dismounted, and tied up their horses to the hitching post. Dude took Maggie's two valises off her horse and they walked into the hotel and up to the lobby desk.

"You speak American?" Dude asked the man behind the desk.

The man smiled and nodded his head, "Si, yes," he responded.

Dude smiled, "We would like your best room, por favor. And we also need our horses taken care of; they're tied up out front."

The man said, "Of course, Señor. Please sign to register," and opened a book, turned it around and handed Dude a pen.

"Maggie loudly whispered to Dude, "If you write 'Mr. and Mrs. Howard Warren' I'm leaving."

Dude turned to Maggie, winked, and said, "Mr. and Mrs. Arthur A. Chester. That'll fool 'em."

#

Their room was elegant, even for hotels back East. The large bed had a gold headboard and the bedspread was made of silk and had a gold floral pattern. On either side of the bed was an oak nightstand with identical white and blue porcelain vases containing marigolds. There was a dressing table made of oak with a gilt-edged mirror. There was a white and blue porcelain pitcher-and-bowl that matched the vases. The two windows in the room were framed by white lace curtains.

When the bellhop placed Maggie's luggage down, Dude handed him a silver dollar and said, "Now could you bring up a bottle of champagne – champán, por favor?"

The bellhop smiled and said, "Si, Señor, inmediatamente."

When the boy had left, Maggie said, "Champagne, Howard? Won't your money run out?"

"First," Dude said, "never call me Howard again. Second, we're celebrating, remember? New lives. New starts. New places. In fact, that reminds me: I need new clothes. All I took was what was on my back and in my pockets. I even left my guns. Maybe we can go shopping later. For clothes, not guns."

Just as Maggie was saying, "You will always be a dude. But we shall see about shopping," the bellhop knocked on the door with their champagne. Dude tipped him another silver dollar.

They drank the champagne and made love the remainder of the day and throughout the night.

Chapter 28

Curtis was hungry, tired and irritated. He was following the map and knew he was getting closer to Rio Bravo, but while he had found enough sources of water, he had had almost nothing to eat. The day before, he had found an apple tree and had eaten his fill but less than an hour later, he had a violent attack of diarrhea. He had found mushrooms and berries but had vomited them up almost as soon as he had swallowed them. His stomach and head ached constantly.

Based on the copy of the map, Curtis figured he was thirty miles or so from La Presa, which meant about fifty miles to Rio Bravo. He was so anxious to make progress that he wished he could continue to ride at night but he knew he would go off course in the darkness. When the sun was beginning to set, he saw smoke from a fire in the distance. He took out George Walsh's spyglass and saw a group of men, perhaps five, making camp. He spurred his tired horse on towards the direction of the fire.

"Hello in the camp," he yelled as he got within twenty yards, "Can I join you?"

A tall man in chaps, wearing a wide sombrero called back, "Si. Bienvenida. Come."

Curtis steered his horse towards the campsite. He saw five men, all Mexican. Two were throwing mesquite brush on the fire and another was busy preparing food in a pot and a frying pan. A boiling pot of coffee lay on a bed of rocks on the side of the fire. Another man was unsaddling each of the horses. The man who called back to Curtis waved to him and said, "Amigo. Friend. Come."

Curtis dismounted and led his horse by the reins. "Hello," he said, "Can you spare any food?"

The man said, "Si, si. Come. Take off the saddle. You can put your horse with ours. We feed you both," and laughed.

Curtis shook his hand and said, "That old donkey don't need nothin'. He's just a nag."

The man stopped smiling. "You must take care of the horse, Señor. Then it take care of you." He turned to the man who was unsaddling the horses. "Luis," he said, "cuidar el caballo del hombre."

The man named Luis walked over and took the reins of Curtis' horse and led him to the other horses. He took off the horse's saddle and blanket and began to rub the horse down with a damp rag. When he was done wiping the horse's neck and back, he wiped down each of the horse's legs and examined the hooves. When he was done, he carried the saddle back to Curtis, who was drinking a cup of coffee with the man he had been speaking with, who sat across from him. "What is your name, Señor?"

"Lomax," said Curtis, "Chris Lomax. I work at the Burdette ranch. I'm the foreman."

The man smiled and said, "Señor Burdette! We know Burdette. Many cattle, many horses. Much land."

Curtis nodded, "Yeah, that's right. You men are dressed like cowboys – vaqueros (he pronounced it "vack-a-rose") – are you vack-a-rose?"

The men exchanged glances and laughed. The first man said, "Si, vaqueros. You Spanish is very good. Yes, we are cowboys."

Another man offered Curtis a tortilla filled with beans. Curtis nodded in appreciation and bit lustily into the tortilla. He finished it in three bites and the man he was speaking with turned to the cook and said, "Mas frijoles por el hombre."

Curtis accepted another tortilla and said, "Are you looking to sign on somewhere? I can get you work with Burdette."

The man smiled and said, "No, gracias. Thank you. But soon we have plenty of cattle ourselves. Not as many as Burdette maybe, but plenty cattle." He looked at the other men and those who understood English laughed.

Curtis did not understand the humor but gave it little thought as he ate the frijoles and drank the strong coffee. He sat back against his saddle.

The first man offered Curtis a rolled cigarette and said, "You going to the ranch of Burdette?" Curtis nodded. The man said, "You have another day's ride, at least."

Curtis said, "Yeah, another day or so. I've done this trail so many times I can do it with my eyes closed. Where are you boys headed?"

The man lay his head on his saddle and put his hat brim over his eyes. "Oh, we are headed south, Señor. Back home." The other men went about building up the fire, cleaning pans and preparing for sleep.

In the morning, the leader of the men woke Curtis by kicking the bottom of Curtis' boot. He handed Curtis a cup of coffee and said, "Buenos dias. We are to go but we have made eggs and leave you more coffee. Good luck to you, Señor. Adios."

Curtis rose and shook the man's hand. "Thanks for everything. If you ever need work, come look me up at the Burdette ranch. Adios." He turned and waved to the other men who were already on horseback. Two of the men returned his wave.

After finishing the eggs and the coffee, Curtis tossed the tin plate and cup into the dying fire, mounted his horse and headed west towards the Burdette ranch.

Feeling refreshed, Curtis was able to ride until sunset, placing him within ten miles of the ranch. He decided to push on and arrived at the ranch sometime after nine o'clock. There seemed to be a party going on at the ranch house. Curtis rode passed the gate and up to the house. He dismounted and handed the reins to one of the attending cowboys standing outside. He walked up the steps and entered the house, failing to take off his hat. A man wearing a white and brown leather vest met him at the door. It was Burdette's younger brother, Joe.

"Just who the hell are you?" asked Joe, who was noticeably drunk. Before Curtis could give an answer, Joe said, "This is by invitation only. And take off your damn hat. What're you, a farmer?"

Curtis, intimidated, took off his hat and said, "I was hired by Nathan Burdette for a special mission. I need to see him right away."

Joe stared at Curtis and said, "Stay right here." He then turned to two men standing behind him and said, "Watch him. Make sure he don't eat, drink or steal nothin'." He then turned toward the crowd of people in the next room and walked away.

In a few minutes, Joe returned with Nathan Burdette. Nathan spoke directly to Curtis. "What's your name?"

Curtis stammered, "Curtis Logan. I was with Chris Lomax's outfit. To rustle the cattle to Mexico."

Nathan Burdette looked around then grabbed Curtis by the arm and said quietly but firmly, "Come with me." They walked to his office. The large desk in the office had a leather blotter, a stand with pen and ink, a box of cigars, a decanter filled with whiskey, and several crystal glasses. There was a fireplace and Nathan Burdette motioned to the man tending to the fire to leave. Over the fireplace was a mounted buffalo head. On the opposite wall was a large map of Texas. The map had a large circle drawn in black pencil around the portion that indicated Burdette's land, with smaller red circles around surrounding areas.

Burdette sat behind the desk and indicated to Curtis to take the seat in front of it. "Would you like a drink?" Curtis nodded and Burdette poured a single glass of whiskey. "So, tell me what happened."

Curtis took a sip from the glass and said, "Well, we got the herd. But we had to kill all them cowboys. Chris wanted to charge 'em but I told him, no, that that wasn't the plan. And them cowboys put up a fight. A bunch of 'em was Texas Rangers. They got a dozen of us until we finally took 'em. They got Chris, too. That's when I took over. I organized it to make it look like a Comanch' raid. Put arrows in ev'body. Ev'body dead, anyway," he smiled weakly. "Then I got the rest to take the herd to Mexico. Like the plan said." He took another drink of whiskey.

Burdette saw his chance to ask questions and said, "How much of the herd did you manage to keep?"

"All of 'em," Curtis said. "Almost all of 'em."

Burdette sat back in his chair and said, "Why didn't you go with the herd?"

Curtis finished what was left in the glass and answered, "Well, I figured someone should get back to you with the news."

Burdette looked at Curtis, "So they're driving the herd to Mexico without your leadership? Do you think that wise?"

Curtis rubbed his chin. He said, "I thought you would want to know right away. I trust them. They the best cowhands in the outfit."

"And you had arrows shot in every dead man? Including Lomax's men? And you are sure that all of Joe Edwards' band are dead?"

"Uh, no, no arrows in our boys," answered Curtis. "I made it look like a battle. And I know all of Edwards' bunch is dead. But you'll like this: I had Joe Edwards stripped and tied to a wagon wheel like Comanch' would do it. Weren't that good?"

Burdette did not answer. He pulled out the top draw in his desk and produced a banded stack of fifty-dollar bills. "What amount did we agree upon?" he asked.

Curtis looked at the stack of bills. "Well, it was fifty a man but since I organized and was one of the survivors I thought maybe more. I had to fight my way back through banditos and all."

Burdette paused. "Okay," he said. "I will give you fifty as agreed and another one hundred for your 'leadership' and survival. When do you think the others will return from Mexico?"

Curtis tried to contain himself in spite of the thought of the one-hundred and fifty dollars that he would possess momentarily. "I'd say a week, maybe two."

Burdette counted off three fifty-dollar bills and said, "I'll make you a proposition: if you remain quiet about your 'mission' I will pay you five percent the proceeds from the sale of the herd in

Mexico. For two thousand head at ten dollars per head, your share could be as much as one thousand dollars."

Curtis could not control his joy. He jumped up out of the chair and grabbed Burdette's hand. "Why, thank you, sir. Thank you!" He picked up the three fifty dollar bills and turned to leave.

Burdette rose and said, "Tell no one. Do you understand?"

Curtis stood holding the door, "Why, yes sir. No one."

Chapter 29

Doctor Lamar Fix walked out of Stumpy Callahan's bedroom and over to Marjory Beavorson, who was sitting in an upholstered wing chair by the fireplace. "Marjory," said Fix, "I've got the fever down slightly but I'm still worried about those stomach problems. I also put some salve on his feet and legs and they seem to be coming along. He's been talking a lot but not making a heck of a lot of sense. At least not to what I can understand. You can come in."

Marjory stood and walked quickly into the bedroom and went to the side of the bed. She stroked Bradford's damp hair and felt the heat within his forehead. "Ma," he said, blinking several times. "Ma. They're not Injuns. They're men. Ma, Taylor is by the stream. Maybe I could've. Taylor. I ran. I'm sorry. Joe. Ma." His eyes were wide open and he stared at her but Bradford did not seem to see her. It was as if he was looking through her.

Marjory quietly soothed her son and whispered, "It's all okay now, Bradford. It's all okay and you rest now." She bent down and kissed his scorching forehead.

Stumpy came in from watering the garden just as Marjory and the doctor were leaving the bedroom. Closing the door behind him, the doctor said, "Believe it or not, up to now that was the most coherent he's been."

Stumpy stood in the front doorway and said, "I can't wait until Diego gets back, I didn't realize how much work this is." Looking at the doctor, he said, "Well, any better?"

Doctor Fix looked at both of them and said, "Let's go to the parlor and sit down."

When they were each seated, the doctor began, "I have to be honest with you. I am using all the methods I know of to bring that fever down but it's like pushing a bolder uphill. There's temporary measures like cold compresses, but they are simply that: temporary. I think there's some type of poison deep down, something he must have eaten or drank on the trail and for the life of me I can't purge him of it. It ignores any purgatives I use. His vomiting doesn't even seem to rid his body of it. It's as if it's clung on to something inside, his organs maybe. Just please know that I'm trying and will continue to try." He paused and looked at each of their faces. "Now," he continued, "that's the medical side. On the legal side, based on the little I'm able to piece together, something disasterous must have happened on that drive. Maybe we should consider bringing in Chance." He looked at them again. "I know you're thinking that Brad may not be up to it and it would take a lot of deciphering to put the real story together, but at this point, I'm worried Brad may be the first – or only – link to it." He looked at their faces again. "Don't worry, I'm not in any position, at this point at least, that I have to report anything to any authority. Maybe I'll just shut up now and let you two have a say."

Stumpy relented to Marjory, who said, "Doc, I know you are doing everything you can for my boy and I appreciate it. If we can help any one of them others and maybe go out and save them, we got that responsibility. If we can have their families find out the truth that's just as important as saving Bradford's life."

Stumpy nodded and added, "Exactly what I was thinking, Marjory. I gotta go into town anyway to check again for a wire from Joe. Then I gotta go to the bank. I can drop in on Chance and tell him. Get him to come out here."

They all agreed to Stumpy's plan and the doctor told Marjory that he would be back in the afternoon and then left in his buggy. Stumpy hitched the horse to his wagon and went into town.

#

That morning, Sheriff John T. Chance had already broken up two fights and arrested two cowhands for public drunkenness and disorderly conduct. He heard that there was a party at Burdette's ranch the night before and some of the cowboys decided to extend the party to the two saloons in town. The Sheriff had to beat one of the cowboys into submission in order to get handcuffs on him. He had placed both cowboys in the same cell. One slept while the other sat on the floor holding his head.

Chance was still dealing with the death of Ned Burke. He knew he had been poisoned, and probably by that woman. But how could he prove it? She and Dude were long gone by now. He did not suspect that Dude had anything to do with it, but if Chance pursued the woman as Burke's murderer, Dude could be implicated as an accessory after the fact. Was Burke worth it? he asked himself.

#

Stumpy walked into the telegraph office next to the bank and went to the wire desk. "Anything today, Michael?" he asked the young man behind the counter.

Michael shook his head and replied, "No, Mr. Callahan. Nothing today either. But I sent a wire to Las Animas office asking to send any word right away and that we would cover all charges from both sides. Mr. Smith said that it would be okay."

Stumpy said, "Thankee, Michael. And be sure to thank Mr. Smith for me, too." He turned and headed to the bank.

#

The President of the Rio Bravo City Bank, Stephen Borris, walked out from his office and greeted Stumpy as if he was expecting him. "Mr. Callahan," Borris said, extending his hand, "Please come into my office."

The walls of Stephen Borris' office were appointed in polished oak panels. There was a painting of the Alamo and another of a sunset over an Indian campground, showing white and beige teepees and smoke from a dying fire. On the wall behind Borris' mahogany desk was a floor-to-ceiling bookshelf containing banking and law books of identical size and color. On the top of the desk was a small bronze statue of a bull, its head thrust up and its horns frozen in an attacking position. Also on the desk was a set of papers, the first page containing the title, "Callahan Real Estate Loan."

"Please be seated," Borris said to Stumpy. "Care for a cigar?"

Stumpy declined the cigar and said, "I see this is about the loan. Well, I wanted to talk to you about extending it. Ya see, the herd hasn't been brought to market yet and…"

He was interrupted by Borris. "Yes, we understand the circumstances. However, the covenants of the loan were – and are – quite clear. The first payment was due within thirty days of the dispersal of the funds to you. It has been almost twice that. An extension, I'm afraid, is quite out of the question. It is my duty to inform you that the bank has begun the procedure of foreclosing on the property referenced in the loan agreement. Unless you can make that first payment, along with the additional accrued interest, right away, we will be forced to begin the foreclosure process."

Stumpy struggled to think of alternatives. "Couldn't I sell the house to raise part of the payment?"

Borris placed both of his hands on his desk and leaned forward. "The collateral for the loan was the land as well as any dwelling already constructed on that land. Quite frankly, the land itself is the real value, not the house."

"But the amount of the loan was for a lot less than the value of the land, according to the bank. Ya said so yerself. What if I were to sell just a portion of the land?" asked Stumpy, anxiously.

Borris leaned back in his chair. "Texas regulation does not allow the arbitrary parceling of land. But more to the point, the loan was against the entire plot as defined in the survey." He began to go through the stack of papers.

Stumpy scratched his beard. "I have some livestock, a couple dozen horses, chickens and such. That should raise part of the first payment."

Borris sighed heavily. "Yes, of course you could do that, Mr. Callahan. However, our estimate of the value of the – your – possessions falls short of the entirety of the principal of the loan itself. The bank considers it a bad risk. The sale of ancillary items, such as the livestock, would only delay the receipt of the first payment. If you prefer, we could deduct the value of the items from the principal loan balance, saving you the effort of finding a buyer."

Stumpy sat back in the chair. "So, this is it? Ya gonna have to take off them fancy clothes and get dirty working a cattle ranch, I can tell ya."

Borris smiled, "The bank is not in the cattle business. In fact, the bank is not in the real estate business either. We are in the business of securing money and lending it out. We will find an appropriate buyer for your land as quickly as we can as it is in the bank's best interest. Please pardon the pun."

Stumpy stared at Borris and said, "It won't take you long to find that buyer, I'm sure. His initials are N.B. and you can sell it to him the next time you're in his saloon." He stood up.

Borris stood up as well and said, "I'm sorry, Mr., Callahan. The bank will inform you when the foreclosure procedure has been executed. You will have thirty days from that time to vacate the dwelling. As a courtesy, I am allowing you to keep all of your personal possessions."

Stumpy quickly thought of those possessions: a pair of maple rockers, a calotype photograph of May-Anne, a gold necklace, a packet of letters from his mother in Ireland, and a drawerful of carvings whittled by his sons over the years. He put his shoulders back and said to Steven Borris, "I think I'll take that cigar now. In fact, make it two. I may run into a friend."

Slightly startled by the request, Borris recovered and said, "Yes. Why yes, of course. Please." He reached into the cigar box and produced two cigars and handed them to Stumpy.

Without thanking him, Stumpy turned and, with his pronounced limp, walked out of Borris's office and bank.

#

Stumpy walked to the jailhouse and entered. Sheriff Chance was sitting behind his desk when Stumpy walked in. "John T., I think I need ya over to my place. Bradford Beaverson is back from the drive. But he's sick, mighty sick."

Chance looked up at Stumpy then glanced quickly over at the two prisoners in the cell. He rose and nodded to Stumpy. "Let's go outside," he said.

Stumpy looked at the two men in the cell and said, "Yeah, that's the other thing: I could use a drink. Let's talk at the Long Branch."

#

When they got outside, Stumpy said, "I'm sorry, John T., I didn't knowd ya had prisoners. Burdette men?"

Chance looked back at the jailhouse and said, "Yeah, I brought them in this morning. I wish I still had someone like Dude to watch 'em. I don't know what they heard but tell me more. Did Brad come back alone?"

Stumpy shook his head, "By himself on one of Pete Gomez's horses. No saddle. No supplies that I could see. Burning up with fever. Doc's been lookin' after 'im but he's outta his head, talkin' nonsense."

They walked into the Long Branch Saloon and up to the bar. "Hey, Dave," said Stumpy, gimme my usual and one for the Sheriff."

Dave poured two glasses of Irish whiskey and placed them in front of Stumpy and Chance. "Let's sit at a table," said Chance.

Chance looked at Stumpy and said, "I'd like to come out and speak with Brad, if I could. Good boy. Maybe I can get him to tell me something. Anything."

Stumpy looked down into his glass. "Better make that sooner better than later," he said. "I just come back from the bank and it looks like that won't be my place in another month. Something about a lein. Well, the bank's leanin' on me something good."

Chance looked at Stumpy, "How much? Can I –"

Stumpy interrupted him, "Thanks, John T., but it's more than an honest man can afford. The worst part is picturin' Burdette on my land. Maybe in my house…" He finished the glass of whiskey and Chance went to the bar for two more.

As he was waiting, a very drunk Curtis Logan stumbled into the bar with two other cowboys.

"I thought I would spread my business around," yelled Curtis to Dave. "Let both drinking establishments share in my good fortune. Besides, why should I give Burdette all of his money back? Drinks on me!" He slammed both fists on the bar and looked up at

Chance. "Even for the law! Never know when I'm gonna need 'im!" He laughed hysterically.

As Dave placed the two drinks in front of Chance, Chance placed coins on the bar and walked back to the table. Curtis turned to him, "Hey, tin badge!" he said. "My money no good? Hey, I'm talkin' to you, big man!" He walked over to the table where Chance and Stumpy sat.

Wavering and using the table for support, Curtis said, "I wuz talkin' to you, lawman…"

Stumpy looked down at Curtis' hands and saw the Claddagh ring on his right pinky finger. "Hey," yelled Stumpy, rising, "Where d'ja get that ring?"

Curtis stood up and looked at the ring himself then pointed his pincky finger at Stumpy. "I got this from an Kiowa squaw. She liked me a lot. A lot. Why? Do ya like it, old man? Maybe ya wanna buy it from me?"

Stumpy grabbed Curtis right hand and said angrily, "That was my mother's and I give it to Joe Edwards. I'm takin' it back!" Stumpy pulled at the ring.

Curtis pulled his hand from Stumpy's grip and stepped back. "Who's Joe Edwards? I never heard of 'im. Maybe he give it to that squaw. For favors." He laughed. "Yeah, for favors."

Stumpy walked around the table and up to Curtis, "That's a damn lie!" he said, and reached for Curtis' right hand.

Curtis stepped back again and said, "You callin' me a liar, old man" and placed his right hand wide over his pistol.

Chance took two steps forward, grabbed Curtis' right hand with his left and punched Curtis, his fist covering Curtis' nose and mouth. Before Curtis fell to the ground, Chance grabbed the gun out of Curtis' holster, cocked it and pointed it at the two cowboys who came in with Curtis. Both men raised their hands then walked quickly out of the bar. Chance turned to Stumpy, "You sure about that ring?"

Stumpy nodded, walked toward Curtis as he was laying on the floor and bent down and pried the ring off of Curtis's finger. Curtis, his nose and mouth bleeding uncontrollaby, allowed Stumpy to take it. Curtis sat up and held his left hand to his mouth and muttered, "Edwards coulda given it to some squaw. Anything can happen on the trail. How do I know where she got it?"

Chance looked down at Curtis. "If you never heard of Joe Edwards, how do you know he was on a drive?"

Curtis looked up and was quiet for a moment, then said, "He give to me when he wuz dyin'. Wanted me to save 'im but them others already shot 'im. Bullets and arrows. I tried to help 'im but it wuz too late. There wuz nothin' I could do for 'im."

Stumpy squatted down next to Curtis, "Who killed Joe? What about the others?"

Curtis turned to Stumpy, still holding his mouth. "I don't know. I just found him on the trail. Kiowas I think. I got there too late. I wuz by myself."

Stumpy and Chance looked at each other. Chance looked down at Curtis and said through clenched teeth, "Mister, you better start telling the truth this minute and tell us what you saw. Even just to save your own skin."

Curtis stood up. "I ain't tell yas nothin! I don't have to and I ain't supposed to." He staggered out of the bar.

Stumpy turned to Chance and said, "Can't ya stop 'im? Hold 'im? Arrest 'im?"

Chance shook his head, "For what? He didn't even pull that gun. As far as stealing, you got the ring back. He said he's spending Burdette money so if Burdette wants him back, it wouldn't take long for them to pay his fine and get him released. No, I think we have a better chance with Brad. At least getting the truth, anyway. I'll ride out to your place. But I don't want to leave those two drunks in the jailhouse alone." He paused. "Say, Stumpy, if you're not going to be a rancher anymore, would you like a job? I'm in dire need of a deputy."

Stumpy smiled and said, "Much obliged, John T., but I don't want your pity. Or your charity."

Chance frowned. "Hell, this isn't either! I don't know anyone tougher than you and you've got a sense of right-and-wrong and a goodness that's rare in most. Besides, you'd be helping *me* out. You'd be showing me pity." Chance smiled and stuck out his hand.

Stumpy returned the smile and said, "Alright, then. Guess I'm starting a new career in the law." The two men shook hands.

"Okay then," said Chance. "Let's go get you sworn in." They walked out of the bar and towards the jailhouse. While they walked, Stumpy took the two cigars out of his shirt pocket and offered one to Chance.

Chapter 30

Dude and Maggie walked back in the room from their shopping spree. The bellhop carried four large packages and a big white hatbox. Dude tipped him a silver dollar and the young man said, "Graciás, Señor Chester," and walked out of the room.

"Well, Mrs. Chester," said Dude, "You've done alright for yourself. You managed to find elegance in this little Mexican town. But I thought we were shopping for me. Speaking of which, where's my package?" He started sorting through the bundles.

Maggie was opening up the hat box. She took out a swoop-brimmed tan hat that had a thin beige veil attached to its brown hat band. On top of the hat was a long ribbon that matched the hat band and could be tied under the wearer's chin. Maggie put on the hat, placed the veil over her face and secured the ribbon under her chin. She turned to Dude and said, "What do you think? Perfect for riding, eh?"

Dude was untying a bottle of tequila from a brown package and looked up at Maggie. "Looks good. But it would look even better if that was all you were wearing," he said.

"Oh," said Maggie, looking at herself in the gilt-edged mirror, "I think you're still drunk from lunch."

Dude opened the bottle of tequila and poured drinks into two crystal glasses. "The guy said this is the smoothest made and I'm gonna hold him to that." He handed her a glass and said, "To us."

They clinked glasses and both drank. "Hey," said Dude looking at the remaining liquid in the glass, "that old Mexican guy was right: this is smoother than Irish whiskey." He poured himself another glass and offered to pour another into Maggie's but she waved him off.

Maggie, back to adjusting her hat in the mirror, said, "You're becoming quite the connoisseur. Irish whiskey, Mexican tequila, French champagne. A long way from beer and 'it's burns like a branding iron.'

Her mocking immitation of Dude irritated him. He poured himself a third drink.

Maggie saw that Dude was becoming cross and said, "But I do want to thank you for all my presents, darling. You're spoiling me." She went over and kissed him lightly on the mouth.

Dude grabbed her around the waist and said, "Thank me harder." He kissed her passionately.

Maggie stepped out of Dude's embrace and said, "Later, I promise. I think I'd like to sleep off my own lunch and then maybe take a bath."

Dude sighed and said, "Okay. Maybe I'll go down to the bar while you nap. I can put it on the Chesters' bill."

Maggie, putting the hat back in its box, said, "You know that you'll have to pay that bill when we check out, right?"

Dude, who was just about to walk out the door, said, "I know that. I've arrested more than one deadbeat for skipping out on a hotel bill. Besides, I still got money. And when that runs out, we have your money."

Maggie turned and put her hands on her hips. "Hold on there, Deputy. *I* have my money, not '*we*' have my money."

Dude closed the door and stepped toward Maggie. "I thought we were in this together," he said.

Maggie became stern, "We are. Or maybe we are. But is that what you want, to be a kept man? Even Randy didn't treat me like that. If that's your intention, let's end this now."

It might have been the drinks at lunch and the four drinks he just had that made Dude confused. He stood for a moment before saying, "No, I don't want to be a kept man. And I sure don't want you to earn money the way you have in the past. That life is over for you. All I got to figure out is how we're going to live once we're settled. I just thought in the meantime…"

Maggie interrupted him, "In the meantime, you thought you'd just live on my money! *My* money. The money I earned entertaining stinking, fat blowhards and any unshaven, disgusting, rough cowhand who could afford it. My money. This was supposed to be my turn. My chance. And it turns out you aren't man enough to provide it." She turned away. She was not crying, she was angry. "Get out!" she screamed.

Dude turned toward the door and left. He walked down the stairs and into the bar that was attached to the hotel. He sat at the bar and the bartender, a slight youth named Miguel, greeted him. "Hola, Señor Chester. What will your pleasure be today?" He wiped the bar with a rag.

Dude looked up and said, "You got Irish whiskey?"

Miguel shook his head, "No. I am sure we do not. I have some whiskey from up North if you want to try."

Dude nodded and Miguel poured a shot from a label-less bottle of brown whiskey. Dude smelled it then tasted it, drinking half of the shot. It burned worse than any liquor he had ever had, even those first drinks years ago. He finished what was left in the glass and the liquor burned his mouth and throat even more. This is good, the pain is good, he thought to himself. It will replace the pain I'm feeling already. I'm not good enough. I can't love. Other than using a gun, I can do nothing. I have nothing. I'm broken. He looked up at Miguel and nodded for another shot.

Dude woke up more than two hours later. When he lifted his head, his face stuck slightly to the bar. His head was aching and mouth felt as if it had spiderwebs inside it. He squinted from the light of the lantern hanging over the bar. He rubbed his head, then his eyes. Miguel had been replaced behind the bar by a large man with a moustache. "¿Como esta, Señor Cheester?" said the new bartender.

Dude used the bar to steady himself and stood up. The bartender handed him a piece of paper, it was the bill for the drinks. "Firme, por favor," said the bartender and handed Dude a pencil. Dude scribbled his name on the paper and walked towards the staircase. He passed the lobby desk and the clerk, said, "Señor Chester, su esposa – your wife – leave already. Do you stay with us more?"

Dude paused as he tried to comprehend what the desk clerk had just said. "Leave," he said quietly, "she left?"

He ran up the stairs and into their room. All of her luggage was gone. All the dresser drawers were open. The packages, including the empty hat box, were scattered throughout the room. He looked around for a note on the all the surfaces, including the bed. He ran downstairs and asked the desk clerk, "Did she leave anything for me, a note, anything?"

The desk clerk shook his head, "No, Señor, she no leave you nothing. Nada. She take your horse, as well. For the equipaje, el luggage."

Dude looked at the floor, his mind racing. "Damn," he said aloud. He looked at the desk clerk. "I need to check out, too, then," he said.

"No problema, Señor Chester," said the clerk. "I get the bill for you." He reached into the cubbyhole that coincided with the number of Dude and Maggie's room and produced a piece of paper containing all charges. He handed the paper to Dude.

Dude stared at the paper. He rubbed his head and face, looked up at the clerk and said weakly, "I – I can't pay this. At least not all of it. Not right away."

The smile left the clerk's face. "That is a problem, Señor. How much can you pay?"

Dude reached into his pockets and produced all the bills and silver he had and laid them on the counter. The clerk sorted through all the money. He looked up and said, "Si, this is not enough. Even with American." He spoke loudly in the direction of the bar. "Jorge, venti aqui."

The large barman appeared in the doorway. The clerk said to him, "Asegúrese de que el gringo no deja." He then summoned the bellboy. "Obtener el alguacil, pronto," he said to the boy. The boy ran out of the hotel and down the street.

The barman approached Dude and stood beside him as the clerk ascended the stairs. The clerk went to Dude and Maggie's room and searched for anything of value. Finding nothing, he left the room and went back downstairs. He looked at the barman, "Nada," he said, disgusted.

The clerk looked at Dude and said, "Maybe you have someone who can send you the money? The money you owe?"

Dude briefly thought of Chance, then shook his head and, raising his hands helplessly, quietly answered, "No."

The clerk shook his head then and replied, "Then, si, yes, this is a problem." He looked up as the bellhop came into the hotel with the local lawman. The lawman was shorter than the bellhop and very stout. He was unshaven and his gray shirt carried a badge with the word "alguacil" inscribed on it. His holster carried a large revolver and he held a black club in his hand. The lawman looked at the clerk and they spoke rapidly in Spanish. While they were speaking, the bellhop leaned on the counter; he seemed to be regarding the scene as entertainment.

The lawman finally turned to Dude and waved the black club at him. "You must go with him," said the clerk. "You go to the jail now."

"For how long?" Dude replied.

The clerk began to gather all the money on the counter. With his head down, he said, "Until the deuda – the debt, your debt – is paid."

Dude became angry, "But for how long?" he demanded.

The clerk shrugged his shoulders as the lawman grabbed Dude's right arm. The large barman walked behind Dude as he was led away by the lawman. The three walked down the street, with the lawman holding Dude by the arm the entire way. They reached the jailhouse, which was situated in the same part of town as the one in Rio Bravo. The jailhouse did not contain a desk or rack of guns. It only had one cell, which was three times the size of the one in the Rio Bravo jail. The cell contained no cots, and there was no window. The three walls were riddled with holes. There were seven prisoners in the cell. One was urinating in the middle of the far wall. Another was vomiting in a corner. Three were asleep on the floor, one in the middle of the cell. The two other prisoners sat across from each other with their knees up. They watched as the lawman unlocked the cell and led Dude inside it. The lawman locked the door behind him. The smell of feces and body odor overwhelmed

Dude and he gagged. He looked at each of the seven prisoners then found an empty spot by the near wall and sat down. The man across from him began to cough loudly, the disturbed congestion rumbling audibly in his chest. The man sitting closest to Dude continued to stare at him. The man who was urinating turned and walked over to Dude. "Juero," he said in a low voice, "Tobacco."

Dude shook his head and looked away. The man kicked Dude's boot with his bare foot and repeated, "Tobacco!" then stuck out his hand.

Dude looked up at the man and said firmly, "No tengo tobacco," but the man went to kick Dude's boot again. In one motion, Dude grabbed the man's foot and turned it inward then pulled it toward him. The man fell on his back and Dude got up and stood over him. "No tengo tobacco!"

The man sitting closest to Dude jumped up and tried to grab Dude from behind but Dude turned to his right and punched the man and he went down. The man who was asleep in the middle of the floor stood up and rammed Dude in the stomach with his head, sending Dude's back to the wall. Dude put both of his hands together and hit the man in the spine then kneed him in the face. The man fell backward, blood pouring out of his nose. The man Dude had punched stood up and was joined by one of the other men who had been sleeping. The two men charged Dude. He hit one in the face with his left fist and grabbed the other by the throat. Dude turned the choking man towards the wall and banged the back of the man's head against it. The man he had just punched, along with the man who was coughing, ran at Dude and grabbed his arms. The man Dude had been choking began to punch Dude in the face and stomach. Dude twisted his body and the blows hit his ribs on his right side. He managed to get his right arm free and dug his fingers into the eyes of the man who was holding his left arm. The man screamed in pain and let go of Dude's arm. Dude then brought his right elbow across, striking the man who was hitting his ribs, across the face. The man who had been holding his right arm only seconds ago tackled Dude to the floor. Dude grabbed the man in a headlock and began to punch his face with his left fist. The man who had demanded tobacco limped over to Dude and began kicking him wildly and unrelentingly in his kidneys and on his spine with his bare right foot. Succumbing to the pain, Dude released the man's head and rolled onto his back. Two of the men pounced on him, striking his head and face repeatedly. Dude was able to kick one off but two more men jumped on him and continued to pummel him. A third joined the pile, grabbed Dude by the hair and smashed his head onto the concrete floor. Eventually, Dude lost consciousness.

When Dude awoke, his eyes were so swollen that he could barely raise the lids high enough to see. His head and jaw ached, and his ribs hurt so much that he could not sit up. The hair on the back of his head was matted with blood and it stuck to the concrete floor. He felt a chill on his feet and looked down to see that his boots were gone. The pockets of his trousers had been turned inside out and one had been ripped completely off.

Chapter 31

When Sheriff John T. Chance rode up to Stumpy Callahan's ranch house, he saw Doctor Lamar's Fix's one-horse surrey stopped in front. Chance dismounted, tied up his bay horse on the hitching post and walked inside. Marjory Beaverson, who had fallen asleep on the upholstered chair in the parlor, woke up when she heard the door close behind Chance. She called to him, "John? Is that you Sheriff?"

Chance hung his hat next to the doctor's on the hat rack, then turned in the direction of the parlor and went over to Marjory Beaverson. "How is he, Marjory?"

Marjory looked into the kerchief she had in her hands and said, "Doc's in there now." She looked up, "Are you here to question him?"

Chance placed his hand on the back of the chair and replied, "I'm going to try. I don't have any tricks. Techniques, I think you call it. I'm just going to ask him straight out to tell me what he remembers. What he can remember." He looked at the closed bedroom door and said, "What he's able to tell."

After a little while, Doctor Fix came out of the bedroom. He looked at Chance and said, "Hello, John. I thought I heard somebody ride up." He looked down at Marjory Beaverson and said, "Marjory, the ipecac I gave him purged everything in his stomach but that fever still refuses to break. Whatever poison or infection he has is either holding on or hiding somewhere." He looked back at Chance. "I suppose you want to see him. Question him. I have to be honest with you, John, I don't know what good it's going to do you. Or him."

Marjory looked up at the doctor, "Let him try, Lamar. For Taylor's sake. And the others."

Chance looked at Marjory and then the Doctor. He slowly turned toward the bedroom and entered. He walked to the bedside.

Bradford opened his eyes and looked up. It took him a moment to focus on Chance's face. Then he smiled broadly and his eyes got very wide. He lifted his head slightly from the pillow. "George," he said weakly. "George, did you get 'em all? Tell me ya got 'em all." He lay his head back on the pillow.

At first, Chance just stared. Finally, he said, "Yeah, Bradford. We got 'em all."

Bradford smiled and closed his eyes. "Good, George. They deserved it. They wasn't Indians. Joe knows. Bastards. Sons a'bitches!" Then Bradford drifted off to sleep. Chance stared at him and after a minute, Bradford opened his eyes and said, "You ain't mad, right?"

Chance shook his head slowly and said, "No, I ain't mad."

The response seemed to have pleased Bradford; he smiled and closed his eyes. He mouthed the word, "Good" and drifted off to sleep again. Chance waited, hoping Bradford would awaken again. He thought about the questions he wanted to ask and how he would go about asking them. Chance pulled a chair up along the bedside and waited. After fifteen minutes or so, Bradford opened his eyes. He looked at Chance. Again, it took his eyes some time to focus. Finally, he said, "I got Burny's canteen. One of 'em give it to me. I'm a good hand now, ain't I?"

Chance stood. He said, "You're right that you're good. Damn good. Best we got." He tried one of his rehearsed questions: "Bradford, where's Taylor? Do you know where Taylor is?"

A look of sadness and confusion appeared on Bradford's face. "By the stream. Y'all know that, Joe. Taylor's by the stream. Y'all know that."

Chance answered immediately, "Yeah, the stream. I forgot." He tried another question: "Who's watching the herd, Bradford?"

The question disturbed Bradford, his closed his eyes tight and shook his head. "Them cowboys ain't no good. They losin' 'em. They don't care. They gonna lose 'em all. They goin' south. Pa's watch told me that." Then Bradford stopped shaking his head and smiled slightly. "George showed me that…you showed me that," he said. Then he was asleep again.

Chance sat down and watched Bradford. After an hour, he stood and left the room as Bradford continued to sleep.

He walked into the parlor. Marjory Beaverson and the doctor were drinking tea. Marjory put down her cup and saucer and rose to speak to Chance. "Anything, John?"

Chance put his fingers through his hair and scratched the back of his head. "As far as Taylor, something about a stream."

Marjory replied, "Yes. He said that to me, too. 'Taylor's by the stream.'"

Chance looked at the floor and said, "Well, when he says it like that, I'm guessing he didn't drown in a stream." He looked at Marjory Beaverson. "Sorry, Marjory. I didn't mean –"

Marjory Beaverson waved her hand at Chance. "No, no. It's okay, John. What else did he say?"

Chance stared at Marjory for an instant and said, "From what I can gather, maybe they got separated near a stream. But it also sounds like the herd got rustled. At one point, he called me 'George' and at another he thought I was Joe. Joe Edwards, probably. I don't know any of the other hands that were on the drive, other than Bradford and Taylor. And Stumpy's man, Diego, was with them." He turned to the doctor, "He's been asleep for about an hour. He's so hot, I can almost smell the fever."

The doctor put down his tea and said, "I'll apply some more compresses," then got up and went to the kitchen.

Marjory Beaverson stood up and Chance said, "I'll try again tomorrow. I don't want to wear him out. Maybe we can piece this thing together. Slowly, over time."

Marjory said, "He may not have time, John. I'm preparing myself for that. I've taken care of their fevers – and their father's – but I never seen one as high or strong as this. But thank you for trying."

Chance nodded, walked to the door, took his hat and left. He rode back to town.

#

When he walked into the jailhouse, he found Stumpy wiping down each rifle in the gun rack. Stumpy looked up and said, "Some of these guns are filthy!"

Chance threw his hat on one of the hooks near the door and said, "I didn't hire you to do that." He took the keys to the cell doors that were hanging on a peg on the far wall.

Stumpy looked at Chance and said, "Do ya have a maid what comes in and does it for yer? I didn't think so. So I thought I'd make it part of my…" When he noticed Chance opening the cell door and letting the two cowboys out, he stopped talking.

Chance held open the cell door and motioned with his thumb for the cowboys to get out. "You're free. Get going," he said. "If there's a next time, it will be for a whole lot longer." The two cowboys rose, looked at Chance, then at each other. They slowly walked out of the cell and then through the jailhouse door.

Once they were gone, Stumpy said to Chance, "Ya let 'em go? But after –"

Chance went over to his desk. "After what they *may* have heard? I can't worry about that now and I can't hold them indefinitely. At least not for drunk and disorderly. Besides, I don't want anyone hearing what you and I have to talk about. Have a seat." He indicated the chair across from the desk. "I spoke with Bradford. I think your herd was rustled. And I think they were driven south. Was there a 'George' in Joe's outfit?"

Stumpy nodded. "George Walsh. He was a Ranger at one point? What about him?"

"Brad mentioned him. Wanted to know if he 'got them all.'" Who would 'Burny' be?"

Stumpy smiled, "That would be Milburn, Alice Palmer's boy. Nice boy, real good hand. Good cook, too. What did Brad say about him?"

"Not much," said Chance. "I think he may have been killed. Maybe by whoever rustled the cattle. Let me ask you, on the trail you laid out, about how many streams did they pass?"

Stumpy scratched his beard. "Oh, I don't know, John T., hard to say. There was a lot, I can tell ya that. We tried to hit as many water sources as we could. When I get back to the house, I can get my copy of the trail map. Why do ya want to know?"

Chance sat back in his chair, "Because I think Taylor Beaverson may be buried by one."

Chapter 32

Four riders came into Las Presas and went up to the only saloon in the town. They tied up their horses and went inside. They stood at the bar and one man ordered a pitcher of beer. The barman brought the pitcher and four glass mugs. "Four bits," he said to the men.

One man placed money on the bar and said, "Thanks. Keep it." The man poured his own beer and pushed the pitcher to the man on his right. "Say," said the man to the bartender, "I'm looking for someone. He may be in town. He's about my height but a lot skinnier. He's got a moustache. Dark, dark hair. I think that may be his brown bay mare outside. Seen anybody like that? He likes to drink. He gets loud sometimes, too."

The barman leaned back and said, "Could be the man who rode in earlier. Threw money around. If he's the one, he's upstairs with one of the women. Last door on the right." He motioned with his chin to the door.

The man who asked the question smiled. "Okay, thanks." He turned to the man on his left. "Maybe come up with me." Then to the other two, "Stay down here." He and the other man went upstairs. The man knocked on the door and called, "Curtis, you in there? Hey, Curtis."

There was a sound of a bed squeaking and then the sound of Curtis saying, "Who's there? Who is that? What you want with me?"

The man called back, "Is that you, Curtis? Burdette sent me. He told me to get you and bring you back. He says he got a bonus for you. The herd was sold. Sold down in Mexico. I'll be downstairs. Come on. Hurry up." The two men descended the stairs and joined the other two.

Curtis opened the door slightly and looked out. He came out slowly. He had a blanket wrapped around his waist and held a pistol in his right hand. He walked onto the landing and looked over the stair railing at the four men below. The man who had knocked on the door raised his beer mug and said, "Burdette says you done real good."

Curtis smiled back and said, "A'course I done! You got the bonus with you?"

The man shook his head and said, "No, he wants to give it to you personally. We's here to fetch ya back to his place. You a hard man to track."

Curtis smiled again and said, "Of course I am," and went back inside. He came out a moment later, fully dressed. He turned back and yelled into the room, "That's enough for you. You weren't that good anyway!" He slammed the door.

He joined the four men at the bar and said, "Can I buy you fellas a drink?"

The man who had knocked on his door said, "No, we gotta get ya back. Burdette told us to bring ya back as soon as possible."

As they walked outside to their horses, Curtis said, "I'm glad you fellas showed up. I'm beginin' to run low on cash."

The five men mounted up and rode out of town. When they were about two miles outside of Las Presas, one of the men said to Curtis, "So you was on that drive to rustle that herd?"

Curtis nodded and said, "Goddamn right I was. I was the leader."

Another man said, "And y'all killed ev'body in Joe Edwards' outfit?"

"Had to," Curtis replied. "They wouldn't give up. They was all Texas Rangers, did ya know'd that? Yessir, we had to kill every last mother's son a'them. I didn't have no choice."

The man who had knocked on the door earlier said, "What about that kid, Beaverson from Rio Bravo way?"

Curtis looked at the man and said, "Yeah, him too. What about 'im?"

The rider who had yet to speak slowed up and rode behind Curtis. He drew his pistol, held it down at his side and cocked it.

"Well," said the first man calmly, "He made it back. You lying piece of shit."

The man behind Curtis shot him in the back of the head. When Curtis fell, the man rode up to the body and fired five more bullets into Curtis, hitting him in the chest and face.

The men rode back to Burdette's ranch, leaving Curtis' body and horse behind them.

Chapter 33

Dude did not know how long he had been in the jail cell. It could have been one or many nights. When the Mexican lawman placed the buckets of stale tortillas and warm, insect-infested water in the cell, Dude did not rise and join the others, who rushed toward the pails. He looked around and counted only three other prisoners. The one who stole his boots had been released. One of the remaining prisoners had two swollen and bleeding eyes, a result of Dude's jamming his fingers into them.

When the lawman came to take the buckets away, he motioned to Dude. Dude slowly rose, using the wall for support. The pain in his ribs made him walk hunched over. The lawman said in his low voice, "Ha sido liberado."

Dude understood the "liberado" part. Liberty. Free. Even though it caused him more pain, he picked up his pace and walked out of the cell. He looked around the jailhouse, hoping to see Maggie, but there was no one there. The fact that she was not there to meet him hurt more than his ribs, his head, or his face. The image of seeing her, of her apologizing to him or even giving him the opportunity to apologize to her, was the only pleasant thing he had thought of since walking into the jail cell. The lawman motioned to the door and Dude limped out and into the street.

The sun shone so harshly on Dude's face that he was almost glad his eyes were nearly shut from the swelling. He looked down the main street of Nuevo Laredo in both directions, trying to decide which way to walk. A man on horseback leading a mule brushed dangerously near him and Dude spun and walked toward the hitching post in front of the jailhouse. Finally, he headed toward the hotel.

The young bellhop was sitting outside the hotel with his back against the wall. When the bellhop saw the shoeless Dude, with holes in his pants and shirt, he pointed and laughed. Dude blushed and became self-conscious. He brushed at the dirt of the jailhouse floor that was on his clothes. The bellhop stood and walked into the hotel. Dude wanted to go follow him and apologize to the clerk and perhaps even ask for a job, even a menial one. He was embarrassed and his shame paralyzed him. He limped over to the spot the boy had occupied and sat down. Maybe if he got some rest, he thought, he could build up his strength to approach the hotel clerk. He lowered his head and dozed.

Dude was awakened by the sound of two well-dressed men who walked passed him, heading for the hotel. They were Americans and one looked down at Dude and stopped. The man considered Dude for almost a full minute. Finally, he reached into his pocket and produced a silver dollar, which he laid at Dude's bare feet.

"Why, that is certainly Christian of you, Earl," said the other man.

The two men resumed their walk to the hotel. "Down on his luck. That's all there is to that," said Earl as he placed his hand on the man's back and guided him into the hotel lobby.

Dude stared at the silver dollar. It was not enough for a pair of boots. It could not buy a horse. He had had boots and a horse before. Those things did not make him happy. Those things by themselves could not bring joy into his life. Dude asked himself, When was I happy? What times in my life did I feel good? What made me feel good? He answered by stating that he could never rely on things, or people, to make him happy. He only had himself. He had to make himself happy. Nothing else. No one else.

Dude picked up the dollar and used the wall to support himself as he stood up. He walked through the hotel and turned left, towards the bar. The desk clerk, busy in registering the two Americans, did not notice him. Dude headed toward the bar. The young barman, Miguel, was behind the bar. When he saw Dude, he smiled and bent down to get the label-less bottle of whiskey from under the bar. He placed a shot glass in front of Dude and said,

"Amigo, where you been?" When he saw Dude's face up close, he added quickly, "¿Que paso? What happened to you, my friend?"

Dude did not return the greeting or try to explain anything. He placed the silver dollar on the bar and indicated for Miguel to pour. Miguel obliged and Dude drank the whiskey in a single, greedy motion. He felt the spreading heat of the liquor on his mouth, his throat and throughout his insides. He felt his body anticipate and welcome the hot liquid, and the burn that would soon relieve his worries. Dude's only concern was to please himself; to not have to rely on anything or anyone else to comfort him. He wanted to set aside all other problems for what really mattered to him. In an effort to rush the process and to bring him to that carefree state, he motioned to Miguel to pour again. The second drink was less painful than the first but more effective. The third, then, would be even more so. I need to get to the point, Dude said to himself, where I will be feeling only the pleasure and none of the hot pain. He motioned for a third drink and Miquel poured the whiskey into the shot glass.

"Pero, no mas," said Miguel. "You necit – need – dinero, Amigo."

Dude drank the third drink as quickly and as lustily as the first. He wiped his mouth, looked up at Miguel and said, "Gracias. Thanks," and turned from the bar. It's enough for now, thought Dude. I feel good, strong. He no longer felt the pain in his ribs and stood up as straight as he could. He walked to the hotel lobby and up to the desk. The same desk clerk was behind the counter. He looked up at Dude and sniffed. "¿Señor?" he said coolly.

Dude felt confident. "Sir, I want to apologize to you for the trouble I caused and I want to make good for it. Across the border, I was a lawman, good with a gun. I can do security for you and the hotel. All I ask is room and board."

The man stared at Dude's face and replied, "¿Lo bueno que un luchador puede ser? ¿Has visto la cara?"

The bellhop was leaning on the front of the counter. He saw Dude's confusion and said, "He thinks you cannot be much of a fighter. Just look at your face." The boy grinned and turned to the clerk for approval.

Dude was insulted but continued. "I need a job. I can do anything. I'll wash dishes. Anything. Like I said, you don't even need to pay me. At least not until my debt's paid. Then we can work something out." He paused. "Por favor."

The clerk turned to the bellhop, "Tomar el borracho a las cuadras."

The bellhop laughed out loud. He grabbed Dude by the arm and said, "Come, I will show you to your room."

Dude followed the youth to the stables, where he handed Dude a worn broom and pointed to an empty stall. The bellhop stuck out his hand as if anticipating a tip. He laughed, pulled his hand away and walked back towards the hotel. As he was walking away, he said, "Buenos noches, Borrachón."

Epilogue

The five Mexican vaqueros who had shared their camp with Curtis caught up to the eight cowboys who were bringing the remainder of Stumpy Callahan's cattle to Mexico. The herd was about to cross the border, twenty-five miles northwest of Ojinaga, when the five vaqueros began to ride after it. One of the vaqueros, the one who took care of Curtis' horse, threw a lasso around the shoulders of one of the cowboys on the right side of the herd. The cowboy was pulled off his horse and he landed on his right shoulder, dislocating it. The cowboy in front of him was lassoed around his neck. The vaquero that roped him dragged the cowboy from behind for fifty yards before releasing him. The leader of the vaqueros, the man who had spoken with Curtis, rode alongside the cowboy who was leading the herd, pulled out his pistol and shot the man in his shoulder and head. The leader then motioned to one of the vaqueros to ride ahead and go after the cowboy riding point. He and the other three vaqueros then rode in front on the herd and slowed it. They each drew their pistols. The four remaining cowboys rode up together to investigate the delay and the vaqueros gave them the option to fight or flee. The cowboys collectively decided to abandon the herd. The vaqueros drove the herd over the border and sold it to a Mexican rancher outside Tabaloapa. They sold the eight hundred remaining cattle for six U.S. dollars per head.

Bradford Beaverson fell into a coma a day after speaking with Sheriff John T. Chance. A week later, he died in his sleep. The entire town of Rio Bravo attended Bradford's funeral. The Reverend Douglas Hamilton spoke at the graveside, saying how brave Bradford was and how strong God must consider Marjory Beaverson as He had placed so many heavy burdens upon her to bear.

The Rio Bravo City Bank foreclosed on Stumpy Callahan's land. The five-hundred acre parcel was sold directly to Nathan

Burdette. There were no other bidders. While the amount of the loan was two thousand dollars, the purchase price was six thousand. Stumpy sold his remaining livestock privately and was able to purchase a small, one-room clapboard house just outside of town. He moved in with the rockers, May-Anne's photo, his mother's letters, and the boys' carvings. He kept May-Anne's gold necklace and placed his mother's Claddagh ring on it.

In early spring of 1885, two hunters from Oklahoma came upon the site of the encounter between the Joe Edwards and Chris Lomax outfits. They saw the scorched wagon and Joe Edwards' rotting corpse that exposed portions of skeleton, tied to one of its wheels. They counted six decomposing bodies in close proximity to one another, and another five scattered within an adjourning area seventy-five yards or so away. The hunters reported the scene to U.S. Calvary representatives at Fort Sill. The Calvary sent investigators to the site who examined the corpses, arrows, and bullet casings. In its official report, the U.S. Calvary determined that the scene was a result of a rogue band consisting of Kiowas, Comanches, and Apaches, perhaps escapees from the reservation in southwest Oklahoma. The absence of any Indian corpses was explained, as "Based on certain evidence, it has been established that [the] attacking band of warriors removed their own dead…from the above referenced site and surrounding vicinitys [sic]." The incident became known as the Cimarron County Massacre.

Dude worked cleaning stables and tending horses for the guests of the El Hotel de Oro. For the first three months, he was paid only in label-less pints of whiskey – one per week – and scraps of food from the hotel kitchen. By the end of the three months, Dude estimated, he had worked more than enough to pay the balance of his hotel bill. When he asked the hotel clerk to begin paying him with cash, in order to eventually be able to buy a pair of used boots, the clerk said the hotel no longer needed Dude's services. Dude hung around Nuevo Laredo, surviving on handouts from strangers, for another year. He spent any money he received at the bar next to the hotel. Dude became known throughout the town and the surrounding area as "El Borrachón."

###

CPSIA information can be obtained
at www.ICGtesting.com
Printed in the USA
BVHW04s1831221018
530915BV00011B/326/P

9 781540 804570